'Cookie is curious and stubborn. the perfect little scientist. Her questions and missions lead to surprising, and sometimes explosive, consequences. Children of all ages will love getting drawn into Cookie's adventures. I recommend this book for families to read together and children aged six to twelve reading alone. You can even try out Cookie's experiments in your own kitchen. Young readers will discover, along with Cookie, that you don't need to be a grown up to be a fantastic scientist. You just need to be curious – and maybe a bit stubborn.'

Katherine Mathieson ←(Not only an actual scientist but chief executive of the British Science Association! What a dream job!)

'It's tough learning how to negotiate friendships, yearning and disappointment, and we need stories like this when growing up to help us learn how to do it.'

Philippa Perry ←(Bestselling author and also a psychotherapist. What a cool word and job. People tell her what's going on in their heads ... My book will tell her a lot about what's going on in mine!)

'I really love the book – it wasn't just funny, it was hilarious!!'
Alathea, age 7

'I absolutely love the book, it is so, so, so funny, amazing and brilliant.'
Flora, age 8

'Cookie is so funny, I just can't even explain!'
Brendan, age 7

'When I finished the book, I just wanted to read it again, because it's exciting, hilarious and gripping.'
Amélie, age 8

'I liked this book because it's funny and its characters are amazing!'
Ilia, age 9

COOKIE

Developed by Konnie Huq and James Kay

First published in Great Britain in 2019 by
PICCADILLY PRESS
80–81 Wimpole St, London W1G 9RE
www.piccadillypress.co.uk

This paperback edition published 2020

A CIP catalogue record for this book is available
from the British Library.

ISBN: 978-1-84812-809-5
also available as an ebook

1

Typeset by Perfect Bound Ltd
Printed and bound in Great Britain by Clays Ltd, Elcograf S.p.A.

MIX
Paper from
responsible sources
FSC® C018072

Piccadilly Press is an imprint of Bonnier Books UK
www.bonnierbooks.co.uk

*For Charlie, Covey and Huxley,
you blow my mind . . .*

COOKIE!

...and the MOST ANNOYING BOY in the WORLD

WRITTEN and
ILLUSTRATED by

KONNIE HUQ

PICCADILLY
PRESS

ABOUT ME!

Name . . . Cookie Haque – well, kind of.*

Parents . . . Abed and Rozie.

Sisters . . . Nahid and Roubi.

Age . . . Nine, although I feel I am more mature than this.

Pets . . . Really want one.

Star Sign . . . Don't believe in all that. I mean, how could somebody's whole personality be determined by random stars or what month they're born in? Makes no sense. E.g. I'm supposed to be a Scorpio but their traits include being jealous, negative, secretive and resentful. I am NONE of those!

> I think Cookie definitely has those traits!

Best friend . . . Keziah, Keziah, always and forever Keziah. BFF.

No. of hours I see Keziah

∞

POSITIVE CORRELATION

my happiness

∞

HAPPINESS GRAPH
(∞ = infinity)

---

*Cookie is actually my nickname. My parents called me কনক (Kanak in Bengali) - from the Sanskrit word for gold - but annoyingly কনক is pronounced more like Konok than Kanak. (Sanskrit is an ancient Asian language by the way.) Anyway, in Bengali it's written with the letters

my current favourite doodle... these hedgehogs

Keziah style one

Hobbies...

I love drawing and doodling. My current favourite doodle is a hedgehog. I like drawing it with different hairstyles. I love long words and chatting too, if you count that as a hobby! I used to collect sachets of stuff, anything really... salt, pepper, shampoo, all sorts – but I've given up on that now. I've collected so many different types of things: coins, stamps, acorns. No idea why I collected acorns. Random!

Favourite Teacher... Ms Krantz

Favourite Subject... Science. How can anybody not love science? I like it because it explains EVERYTHING. It's thanks to science that human beings can build buildings that don't

---

Kaw (⟅⟄) and Naw (⊤), so really in English it should be written as Kawnawk which, said at the right speed, sounds more like Konok than Kanak but they spelled it Kanak as it looks more like Kawnawk! So people started calling me Kanak instead of Konok. Lost yet? Don't be! Because of the confusion this caused, everyone just calls me Cookie!

fall down, design cars and planes that don't crash and make medicines to help us get better. Without

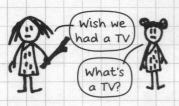

progress in science we'd all still be cavemen running around in rabbit skins with sticks! No houses, no TVs, no iPads! We owe science A LOT.

Favourite Food . . . I love all food except for pork. We don't eat pork in my family cos we're Muslim. My favourite sandwich is coronation chicken and my favourite food at the moment is a roast dinner but it changes all the time. I just love food!

Favourite Colour . . . Favourite colour for what? Just because I like wearing green clothes doesn't mean I want to paint my house green! What a dumb question!

More Stuff About Me . . . I do a good Bart Simpson impression.

CHAPTER 1

Animal Lover

If I don't get a pet soon I'm going to explode. It's taking over my life.

I'm an all-or-nothing kind of person and sometimes when I get an idea in my head there's just no shifting it, and right now I **NEED** to have a pet. Plus, everyone else seems to have one.

Suzie Ashby (the most irritating girl in our class) has **FIVE**. At least she did on my last count, and I don't even have **ONE**. I didn't really think I was into animals, but then last month I was walking home from school when a random cat snuzzled me in the street. It came over to me (yes, me!) and rubbed up against my legs, then purred loudly before walking off. I was **GOBSMACKED!!** Animals don't usually like me much (and to be fair I'm a bit cautious of them myself, especially big birds).

Ever since that moment, though, I've wanted a pet. Preferably a cat. I've even chosen one in the local pet shop. I've called her Bluey on account of her

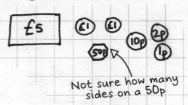

Not sure how many sides on a 50p

huge blue eyes. She costs £150, which I know my parents would never splurge out on for a cat, so I've started saving up. So far, I have £7.63. It's a start.

Big birds terrify me. I quite like the idea of a cute little budgie or fluffy yellow canary, but anything bigger? No thanks. I once got chased by a swan

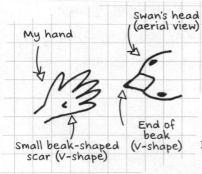

My hand

Swan's head (aerial view)

End of beak (V-shape)

Small beak-shaped scar (V-shape)

when eating a sandwich in our local park and it has scarred me for life. Quite literally. It pecked my hand, leaving a tiny beak-shaped mark on it.

I could never be a hand model on a moisturiser advert now. Thanks a bunch, swan. I had to lob the sandwich (coronation chicken – my favourite sandwich filling) into the pond to get it off my case.

Have the sandwich!

Afterwards I had scary swan dreams for weeks, where they would just come out of nowhere and chase me.

Anyway, back to Bluey. I just think that it would be so nice to have something warm and fluffy to cuddle while watching telly on the sofa. Between you and me, I've actually started pretending my old mohair cardigan is a cat and have been cuddling it in a catlike manner. I even pretended to feed it once from an old plastic bowl I used as a baby.

OK, I *am* aware how crazy this is all sounding, but it just goes to show how badly I need a pet. Maybe something is lacking in my life and a pet will fill the void.

Things that may be lacking in my life . . .

1. My parents won't let me go on ANY social media. Suzie Ashby has her own Instagram account with nearly fifty followers. You're not even supposed to have Instagram until you're thirteen but her mum set it up for her. She constantly posts photos of food she's eaten, clothes she covets and, oh yeah, her gazillion pets. I would be happy with just the one.

SUZIE'S INSTAGRAM

42 followers

Suzie's food

Suzie's wardrobe

Suzie's pets

2. A younger sibling. I have two older sisters and continually get bossed about.

Cookie, can you bring me my bag? And my slippers?

And a hot chocolate choco-latte with extra marshmallows?

Can I do it in a minute?

Now would be better

Thanks!

Being the youngest also means getting all their hand-me-downs. No one would be interested if I had an Instagram account full of pictures of me in my third-hand bobbly jogging bottoms.

COOKIE'S INSTAGRAM

0 followers

crumbs

Cookie's food

Third-hand bobbly jogging bottoms

Cookie's wardrobe

cardigan/cat

Cookie's pets

I would dearly love a younger brother or sister to boss about who would look up to me and wear *my* old clothes.

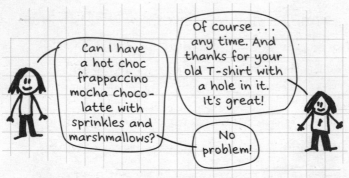

Can I have a hot choc frappaccino mocha choco-latte with sprinkles and marshmallows?

Of course . . . any time. And thanks for your old T-shirt with a hole in it. It's great!

No problem!

3. OK, I can skirt the issue no longer, and so for the last and final void. **Keziah, my best friend in the**

whole world, is leaving. One of her dads has got a job in Solihull and they're moving at the end of term, which is SO hideous I cannot even begin to go into it. 'Void' is not the word; 'chasm' is more accurate.

KEZIAH

CHASM = huge gaping hole in the surface of the planet

I'm no longer going to have my partner in crime. Me and Keziah are SO on the same wavelength: we have the same sense of humour, like the same stuff and often even think the same things – we are kindred spirits! Plus, she's not allowed a mobile phone either, so we can be oblivious of cool apps and social media together.

Keziah is leaving . . .

Woe is me

WAAAAHHHH!

Swans aside, my worst nightmare has come true. Why Solihull? Why not the other side of town? Why not a few roads away? Why not next door to me? I hadn't even heard of Solihull before this. Keziah reckons it'll be much worse for her, and that she'll have to go to a new school where she won't have any friends. I pointed out that I won't have any friends either once she's gone. It's not that I'm unpopular or anything; it's just I've always felt like I don't quite fit in and there's no one else I really want to hang out with. When Keziah joined school at last all that changed. But now, just two and a bit years later, she's leaving.

I googled Solihull and it was named 'Best Place to Live in the UK' in a quality-of-life survey, so not rubbish at all. Great . . . Keziah is leaving me behind, while she goes off to her brilliant new life in the best place to live in the UK.

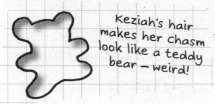

Keziah's hair makes her chasm look like a teddy bear – weird!

So, I'm gonna need to get a pet to fill the Keziah-shaped chasm. Here are my options . . .

Cat – dream pet. Have even chosen one. They are just like cuddly toys that you feed and that sometimes poo on your bed.

I don't poo on beds

Bluey

Though Bluey is far too adorable to soil my duvet. She is just sublime. LOVE her and her BIG eyes.

Currently too expensive so that rules that out for now.

Dog – WAY too much maintenance. I would have to walk it every day. I find it hard enough to exercise myself, never mind a whole other animal.

Come on, you're getting fat – I'll take you for a walk

Yuck!

Fish – this is the only thing I reckon my parents might go for, but you can't really cuddle them on

the sofa without a) getting
soaked or b) suffocating
them to death or c) both.

**Hamster/mouse/other
random rodent –**
Keziah had mice
in her house last year. They
nibbled holes in the pocket lining of
her favourite coat when she
accidentally left a KitKat in it
and they did little black poos
everywhere. Gross! The council
had to get rid of them and it took
weeks. Extremely off-putting.

Bird – a small one obviously. Suzie Ashby has a
budgie that flies around her house and sometimes
sits on a perch in the
corner of her bedroom.
Apparently it likes
listening to classical
music.

I know all this from Suzie's Instagram, which Nahid found for me. Nahid is my eldest sister, who's currently at uni. She's ALWAYS on social media.

I reckon I may have a realistic shot at a bird. Mum is always commenting on birds: their singing, how pretty they are, how they eat the rice she puts out for them in the garden. Who knew birds like rice?

Apparently Mum used to give them leftover rice all the time when she was growing up in Bangladesh. I'm not sure how cuddly a bird would be on the sofa, but here's hoping.

Bird wins. I'll get a bird. A pet will never replace Keziah, but I want one anyway. Maybe it will begin to mend my broken heart.

But how do I get my hands on a bird? Hmm . . .

CHAPTER 2

Annoying Birds

OMG What have I done?! There's a bird in our house. A massive, gross, ugly pigeon with scary stare-y eyes flapping its wings and scattering its feathers all over my living room. Argh! It's about to knock all my mum's plates off the wall. (I mean, who puts plates on a wall when they are clearly for eating off?!!)

My middle sister, Roubi, is
supposed to be 'babysitting'.
Can I just point out, I am **NOT** a
baby. In fact, I'm about eighty per
cent more mature than her. She's

ROUBI

upstairs and oblivious, probably 'being political' or
something, cos that's what she's into . . .

POLITICS??!!! I know. Told you I was more
mature. Anyway, I gotta get this bird out because
my parents will be back any moment and they'll kill
me. This is a disaster and it's all my fault.

You see, there was some leftover rice stuck to
the bottom of the pan from lunch and that's when
I had the brainwave. I'd use the rice to lure a cute
little house martin or some other small bird into the
living room. A house martin sounded ideal as the
word 'house' makes it seem domesticated – perfect
for living in my bedroom.

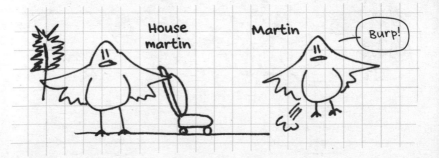

House
martin

Martin

Burp!

The bird would then see how kind I was and this would be the beginning of a beautiful friendship. Maybe I could even adopt it? Or rather, keep it. There's no paperwork necessary with wild animals, I guess.

> Pass the popcorn

I put the rice down and immediately some sparrows flew over and started pecking at the patio. Surely one of them would eventually follow the trail up the step and into the living room? Rice is pretty much the staple diet in our house. Not on its own but with different curries, which means there's lots of variety. Imagine having the same food **EVERY DAY** – life would be so boring. I always think that when I see sheep eating grass in fields alongside the motorway.

> What would you like, sir?

> Have you got anything other than grass?

> No!

> Yum

(You might think sheep are too dumb to care about food. Wrong! Apparently they're really intelligent and can recognise a face for up to two years, and not just one face but **FIFTY** different faces. Not even humans can do that. My mum can barely recognise mine; she calls me by my sister's name half the time!)

Hi, I think we met at Dave's BBQ two years ago

Yes, probably. I forget — so sorry, I'm terrible with faces

Anyhow, just as the birds were polishing off the last of the paving-stone feast, I sneezed (typical!) and they all flew away. Ugh. Now I'd have to put more rice down. But no! Next thing I know, from out of nowhere, this humongous pigeon swoops down, ignoring the rice, and flies straight into our house.

STRAIGHT INTO OUR HOUSE!!! Oh no!!! There's an actual bird in our living room!!! What now? Catch it? How do you catch a bird? I guess I need a long net. We do have a plastic basketball

hoop and stand thing, but obviously with a gaping
great hole in the net, so not much use.

I decide to sneak a look
through the window to
see what it's doing and to
my utter disbelief it is sitting
on the sofa watching TV.
Unbelievable!

It's transfixed! Glued to *Antiques Roadshow*
like a little old man.

Actually, it kind of
looks cute. Maybe I'm
warming to this telly-
watching feathery
fella after all? Perhaps
this pigeon could be
my new pet?

My mum likes birds. What is it she always says about pigeons again?

Oh yeah . . . I forgot. Mum likes all birds *except* pigeons. She calls them flying rats, the vermin of the bird world.

I need to hurry up and get the pigeon out before my parents get back. I head towards the house on a mission. I can kiss goodbye to any form of pet if they get wind of my little rice scheme and the resulting pigeon caper. Donning my bike helmet for protection and wielding my bike pump menacingly,

I stride into the living room . . .

. . . only to find the sofa is now **EMPTY!**

Phew, I think, *it's flown away.* But I think it too soon. I look up – and there it is, sitting on the light shade, frozen still, staring at me with glazed eyes as though it is stuffed. It clearly figures if it stays still long enough it will become invisible. Scared stiff, I too am standing dead still just staring at it. We are now facing each other in some bizarre Mexican stand-off/stare-off competition.

'We're back!' call out my parents. **OH GREAT**. 'Cookie! Roubi!'

STARE-OFF COMPETITION

On hearing them, the startled pigeon starts flying crazily around the room. It's terrified, its eyes bulging with fear. Before I know what is going on, it has circled the room three times, narrowly missing the plates on the wall. It's frantically searching for an escape route and finding it hard to tell which bit of the patio door is glass and which bit is open to the outside world.

Finally, it picks the right side and swoops out into the garden, and that is that. No vases broken, no surfaces scratched, nothing. Although it has shed

half its weight in feathers
in the process . . .

I run to the door to
stop my parents coming
into the living room
before I've had the chance to de-feather it.

'Hi, Mum, hi, Dad!'

'Hi, Cookie!'

Phew! I've got away with it.

'Why are you wearing a bike helmet?' asks Mum.

'Why is there poo on your head?' asks Dad.

'Ha ha, good one!' I say, thinking he's joking, just
as a bit of thick, white yoghurty liquid slides down
a coil of my hair like it's on a helter-skelter slide.

JUST GREAT.

'Don't worry, bird poo's
good luck,' he reassures
me, cracking up as if
it's the most hilarious
thing he's ever seen in
his life.

Actual belly-laughing from my own father. SO
humiliating. I make a point of storming off and
slamming the patio door, but then realise I don't

want to be in the garden, so have to storm back
in past my parents and upstairs. **EVEN MORE**
humiliating. Mum shouts up that I need a bath and
Dad adds, 'Yeah, a birdbath!' Dad's jokes are so not
funny. **SO. NOT. FUNNY.**

Bird poo is good luck indeed! If it *is* lucky, the
luck has probably been used up already by me
having a helmet on, so I need to find some *new* luck
to help me get a pet.

Later, after I fill
my parents in, Mum
is totally grossed out
at the idea that a
disgusting pigeon has
been in our living room.

Meanwhile, Roubi has slept through the whole
thing. Incredible! Apparently she
had been up all night watching
the results of some by-election
or something. YAWN!

Talking of sleep, I haven't
been sleeping that well since I heard Keziah
is moving. The last thing I need right now is scary
pigeon dreams.

CHAPTER 3

The Disappearing Caterpillar Brothers

Unbelievable!

I no longer want a bird. **NO WAY**. Back to plan A – I want a low-maintenance, independent, cuddly cat. A cat won't poo on me from a great height. Hopefully.

After my shower I collapse onto the now feather-free sofa just in time for *Brainbusters*, my favourite TV quiz show. Mum has done a total clean-up operation on the living room and has made me a hot chocolate. I thank her and snuggle up on the sofa.

On *Brainbusters* two teams compete to win prizes for their school. I'm a bit of a quiz-show geek and

I get a buzz trying to answer the questions before the contestants do. (Get it?! Buzz? Quiz shows have buzzers – ho ho!) I often daydream that me and Keziah go on the show and make it to the final and win loads of prizes for the school and then suddenly we're really popular and everyone **LOVES** us. In the dream, Mrs Mannan even apologises for misjudging us all those times she's told us off for chatting in class.

Mrs Mannan was our class teacher last year but when we go back after this summer holiday we should get a new one, hopefully Ms Krantz. I like Ms Krantz cos she always smiles at me and she's a Ms, which is cool. Just like you don't know if a Mr is married or not, a Ms can be a Mrs or a Miss, so it adds a bit of mystery. (Get it?! Ms? Ms-tery? Ho ho!)

No more Mrs Mannan means no more **Catty** and **Pillar**. You see, Mrs Mannan has a moustache – well, a kind of moustache. It's basically a collection of fine hairs that sprout from either side of her mouth like two delicate little caterpillars. The funniest thing about them is that they're there one day but disappear the next, as if she notices them every so often and plucks them out. Sometimes they're replaced by a collection of little dots, which means she's shaved them rather than plucked them.

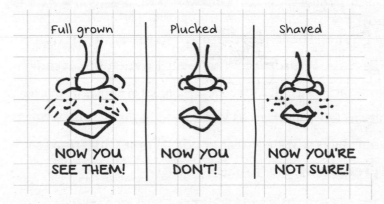

We call them the mysterious disappearing caterpillar brothers, Catty and Pillar, and sometimes talk about them like they're our friends in front of Mrs Mannan and she has absolutely no idea what we're talking about. So funny. OK, maybe you have to be there, but we find it funny.

It's a me and Keziah thing, I guess. There's so many 'me and Keziah' things.

When she leaves there are so many things that I'll miss. **Waaaah!!** Whenever I remember, it makes me sad. I'll really miss her. At least we have a whole term left together, as she leaves in December when her dad's work contract ends. **Worst Christmas present ever!**

Anyway, back to *Brainbusters*. 'Which "C" is in charge of Her Majesty's Treasury?' Chancellor! Chancellor of the Exchequer! **SO** obvious! I could tell even Maddy, the *Brainbusters* host, was exasperated that the boy answered 'treasurer'. 'Treasurer' begins with a 'T'!! His brain has gone bust!! (Get it? Brain gone bust! The show is called *Brainbusters*? Ho ho!) Either that or he's just **VERY** nervous . . . All those cameras on him and a studio audience watching, with his teachers and parents most likely there too, heaping on the pressure. Poor boy. Maybe he shouldn't have worn a T-shirt with the word '**WINNER**' written on it!

This T-shirt may have been an error of judgement

'What "B" is the colour of the flag of the European Union?'

Blue! **BLUE!** The flag of the European Union is blue! He doesn't know the answer. He just said taupe! What colour even is taupe?! And it begins with 'T', not a 'B'! What is *with* this boy? How did he get on this show? How is he in the final? Shame he can't hear me shout the answers at the TV; he'd have won by now. Maybe . . .

I hardly ever win anything. I never win competitions or prizes at funfairs or medals on sports day. One year I *almost* won the egg-and-

1) Arm at right angle to body
2) Spoon like extension of arm
3) A light easterly wind of 1cm per hour reducing drag force

spoon race. I don't know if it was due to my technique or the curvature of my spoon or favourable wind conditions or something, but no matter how fast I went, the egg just didn't budge from my spoon, almost as though it had been glued on.

But just as I was about to cross the finishing line, I tripped over a shoelace and fell flat on the spoon, getting egged in the face in the process. I can remember it so clearly: egg white, yolk, bits of grass and shell blurring my vision as I watched from ground level

Cookie, move! Why are you lying on the grass?

and everyone else's feet went past my nose.

I don't get to see the end of *Brainbusters* as my dad decides to drag me off to the Cash and Carry.

Pretty sure that boy wouldn't have won anyway
with all those wrong answers and passes. No
suspense there. I say 'drag', but I actually love the
Cash and Carry. It's like a giant supermarket where
you buy everything in bulk,
so shop and restaurant owners
(like my dad) can get stock.
Instead of shopping trolleys

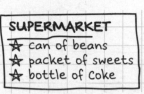

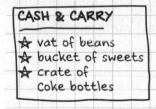

you have airport trolleys,
the shelves are stacked
up high to the ceiling and
all the goods get moved
around on forklift trucks.

Everything is larger in the Cash and Carry.

I tell my dad I will only come if we can go by the
pet shop on the way home and to my total surprise
he agrees. I think it is a compensation measure
for laughing at me so much earlier. He can tell
he's really ruffled my feathers! (Get it? Ruffled my
feathers? Pigeons have feathers! Ho ho!) Perhaps
I can convince him the only *real* compensation
measure would be if he bought Bluey for me . . .

CHAPTER 4

Bluey

Ms Krantz is in the cash and carry! What's she doing here? She's in the sweet section (the best section). There are buckets of cola bottles stacked up next to tubs of gummy bears and there's a gap in between them so I can see through into the next aisle. She's getting a bucket of marshmallow Flumps. Wow! She is such a cool teacher. Knowing her, she's probably gonna dish them out one by one to each member of her new class at the start of term as a welcome present. What a nice touch! Can't wait!!

It's so strange seeing teachers out of school. She is wearing normal civilian clothes: a baggy oversized hoody, leggings and trainers. Very 'un-teachery'. She looks more like a celebrity in a paparazzi shot when they're in scruffy 'no make-up' mode, but look cool anyway. Don't want her to see me or Dad. That would be a bit weird. Teachers are for school life, not normal life – the two worlds don't mix. Plus, it's kind of fun spying on her.

Wonder what *else* she's buying? Can't see from here if she has a trolley. Gonna follow her and find out more. Is she alone? If not, who's she with? Is it her husband? Do they own a shop? What does it sell? Does it sell cereal? Does she have sugar in her cereal? Does she have sugar in her tea? Does she even drink tea? Or is she a coffee person; if so, cappuccino or espresso? Does she pick her nose?

What does she do with the bogeys? Does she use emojis?  *So many questions!* I quite fancy myself as a private detective.

She is walking with purpose; I am hot on her heels. Something catches her eye and she turns around to look. I quickly duck out of the way behind a mountain of Turkish

Delight. (I'm not a fan. I like chocolate and I like jelly, but **NOT** together in the same mouthful.)

 She's looking at a sign about made-to-order cakes. Perhaps she's having a party. She seems like the type that would throw lots of parties. I reckon she has **LOADS** of friends; maybe some of them are even famous. There's probably a chef who cooks the food and an outdoor area with sofas and fairy lights. Maybe even a chocolate fountain to dip fresh fruit and marshmallow Flumps in. Yes, that's it – the Flumps are for the party.

I bet Ms Krantz throws the coolest parties.

She turns back. Looks like she doesn't want
a made-to-order cake on this occasion. Phew,
she doesn't see me. She's walking with purpose
again. I'm right there behind her and, before I
know it, she's striding towards the checkouts, past
the queue, past the cash tills, past the security
guard and . . . *straight out of the shop!* Wha—?
I am dumbfounded. Ms Krantz is taking the
Flumps WITHOUT paying. **MS KRANTZ IS A
SHOPLIFTER!!** No way!! There is a security guard
by the exit doors and she strides right past him
with complete
confidence!
She is even
smiling at him.
How brazen!
Unbelievable.

Wait till I tell Keziah. Krantz has gone way down in my estimation. Thief!

Did I imagine the whole episode? I just saw my favourite teacher shoplifting, and not just any old thing but a whole bucket of marshmallow Flumps. Don't get me wrong, it's better than a gold watch or a laptop, but it's much worse than taking one marshmallow Flump from the pick 'n' mix. That would be small time. *This* is medium time.

I need to assess my options.

1. Tell the security guard. Hmm. But then they'll detain her, call the police and she'll get taken away. She might get a

record and it would ruin her life – all for a bucket of sweets.

2. Wait till school starts and she tries to give out the stolen goods to the class, then tell the head. But it would be my word against hers and no one would believe a pupil against a teacher. She might even try to frame me.

3. Let her know that I know by subtly mentioning Flumps to her **ALL THE TIME**. That will play with her mind and freak her out. And the guilt will be her punishment.

In the end I decide to do nothing. What's a bucket of Flumps in the grand scheme of things? I'm more than sure this is a blip rather than a regular occurrence. Even after I find my dad I can't stop thinking about it. What if she stole other stuff too? Valuable stuff. How do I know there weren't stolen jewels hidden in her hoody? Maybe that's why she was wearing a hoody.

BAGGY HOODIE

watch

gold nuggets

phones

diamonds

Hood up for more complex thefts.

I have failed as a detective. The shame. I feel a bit glum now in the knowledge that my favourite teacher is a petty criminal. Worse still, for all I know she could be an international jewel thief.

The Flumps theft may have just been cos she felt a bit peckish. Maybe she just needed a sugar fix before planning her *next* big heist.

BANK OF ENGLAND JOB
1. Smile at security
2. go to vault, get £
3. Smile at security, exit building

Flump

These Flumps are so good

Flump bucket

Dad must notice me looking glum because he offers to buy me a slice of pizza. Well, that is something I *won't* pass up. I choose mushroom because the only other option is pepperoni, which we don't eat as it's pork. Although to tell you the truth I'm going through a phase where I'm trying not to eat so much meat in general. The fact that sheep recognise faces and I want a pet makes eating meat feel a bit hypocritical.

Keziah and her dads have always been vegetarian and at first I was like, 'What?! You've

BLUEY

You won't eat me, will you?

never had a coronation chicken sandwich? You are missing out . . .' But it's kind of annoying when people say that to me about bacon. And so I've learnt you don't miss something you don't have. I don't miss eating swan or guinea pig or squirrel because I've never even *tried* them.

squirrel   swan   guinea-pig   mushroom

NO GOOD ON PIZZA   GOOD ON PIZZA

Suzie Ashby ate snails in the South of France once. I heard her bragging about it to her best friend, Alison Denbigh. I mean, snails are basically slugs with shells. And you don't eat the shells so basically she ate slugs. Hardly something to brag about, but Suzie could brag about doing a poo if she put her mind to it . . .

It just slipped out of my bum and smelt of roses

Once Dad has got everything he needs for the restaurant, he keeps his promise and we stop by the local pet shop. It's called *Woof, Miaow, Squeak* and it's always a bit smelly – a whiffy combination of sawdust and hamster poo. But it's well worth it because of Bluey. Bluey is the most gorgeous kitten in the whole wide world; she has a glossy black coat and the most magical piercing blue eyes with four soft white paws and a fluffy white tip on her tail to match. Adorable. I always make a beeline straight for her, past all the other animals . . .

She always looks happy to see me. I've visited her throughout the summer holidays, practically since she was born, in fact, and one day she **WILL** be mine. I'm just not sure how. I try convincing Dad on the way here and get the usual lecture about pets being messy and needing constant looking after

and how he and Mum are too busy to do that when
I've given up cos the novelty's worn off.

NOVELTY?!! Bluey is not a novelty. She'll never
'wear off'. She'll be my new best friend once Keziah's
gone. I head towards Bluey's cage, but before I
can even stroke her through the bars a boy with
browny-blond hair swept to one side as if he's in a
boy band barges past me and straight over to her.

'Here he is, Mum!' he cries out excitedly. 'Meet
Nigel!'

Nigel?! Huh? For one thing, Bluey's a *she,* not a
he! And who calls a cat Nigel? It's like calling your
hamster Stuart or your dog Margaret. It's not a
pet name; it's a person name! And besides, Bluey
is MY cat. I want to lie and say, 'Stop! There's been
a mistake. I've already put down a deposit. I'm
just waiting for her bed and scratching post to be
delivered and then I'm taking her home.'

But it isn't true, so I don't. Instead I just watch

as Bluey is stolen away from my life forever – right in front of my eyes. It all happens so fast. The boy and his mum seem so happy and pleased with themselves. I feel so sad and forlorn.

Keziah is going, Ms Krantz is a shoplifter and now Bluey is gone. Forever. And then Dad starts calling me from the front of the shop and pointing at his watch so I have to go.

I knew that bird poo wouldn't be lucky.

CHAPTER 5

Cat Burglar

The first day of term is always annoying. After six weeks of no routine, no assemblies, no lessons, no teachers, no homework, no uniform, you're just thrown back into it like

the summer holidays **NEVER** happened. Like they were all just one lovely long dream.

They don't ease you in. You can't just do every other day for the first week to get you back into the rhythm of it. Nope. It's more like . . . **BOOM!** You're back good and proper. Full days, Monday to Friday, until half-term – a full six and a half weeks away!

Amost two months! **AGES!** Although it doesn't feel like ages when I remember half term will be the halfway point to losing Keziah. First Bluey, then Keziah. No wonder I don't feel like getting up.

Why do the ones I love always leave me?

Can't believe I make it in on time. Waking up is a feat in itself, prising my eyelids open at the seven o'clock alarm call, my head so heavy with sleep it feels surgically attached to the pillow.

When I do finally make it in everyone is catching up with each other excitedly in the playground, clutching their brand-new school bags and wearing shiny new shoes. Suzie Ashby has obviously been somewhere hot. Either that or her dad has bought shares in a spray-tan company.

SUZIE ASHBY

Axel (or to give him his full name, Axel 'I can't bear eye contact with anyone and always look at the floor' Kahn) has had all his hair shaved off. Lots of people have got new haircuts, but his is pretty drastic. He used to have big curly locks that made

him look like a cherub
and now he looks like
he's about to join the
army or something.

AXEL KAHN
(BEFORE)

AXEL KAHN
(AFTER)

Keziah isn't back yet. Her dads booked an
all-inclusive holiday with flights returning this
weekend because it worked out two hundred
pounds cheaper. School is really strict on missing
days in term time for anything other than illness, so
apparently they're going to pretend their flight was
cancelled and
rescheduled by
the airline.

I'm the only
person who
knows and I've
got her back. I'm
gonna save her a
seat and get her any
handouts or homework she needs.

The playground whistle goes and we all shuffle
into Sparrowhawk classroom. All the classes at our
school are named after birds. No Pigeon or Swan
class, though – thankfully. The Year Five and Six

classes are named after birds of prey. Thieving Krantz usually takes Sparrowhawk class, which I was quite looking forward to until now. How can I look her in the eye with the knowledge of the real her beneath that fake nicey-nice exterior? I brace myself.

'Settle down, class, settle down!' booms Mrs Mannan over the classroom hubbub.

Huh? Mrs Mannan? Wha—?

'I have been assigned as your class teacher again, you lucky lot.'

No way! Two years in a row? I have to endure another ten months of her monotonous voice blah-ing on about punctuality, manners and not talking in class. *Yawn!*

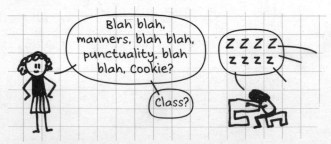

At least she's on the right side of the law, I guess.

'I have some announcements to make,' she announces.

Why announce you have announcements? Just get to the point and announce them. Can't she slip them in with the rest of her chat instead of 'announcing' them?

It is all really boring stuff like the fact lost property is now next to welfare instead of by the main office, and unpaid library fines will double to £6, and other equally unexciting bits and pieces. A proper announcement would be something like 'I'm having a baby' or 'I'm becoming a monk' or 'I'm moving to Timbuktu', not any of the stuff Mrs Mannan is going on about.

I'm beginning to zone out when the most unexpected and brilliant thing happens. Mrs Mannan makes an **ACTUAL** announcement. She announces: 'The school has been successful in its application to be represented on the popular TV quiz show *Brainbusters*.'

NO WAY?! **AMAZING!!!!**

Maybe the bird-poo luck has come good! According to the guidelines of the show, two children will be selected from Year Five – my year! She will give out all the details after lunch. A murmur of excitement spreads throughout the class. How brilliant is this? Me and Keziah could be on TV if we play our cards right. Life is taking a turn!

All I can think about now is *Brainbusters*. There are thirty children in the class, sixty in the year, and two that would be chosen, so I have a one-in-thirty chance.

$$P(BB) = \frac{2 \text{ (no. contestants)}}{30 \binom{\text{no. in}}{\text{a class}} \times 2 \binom{\text{no.}}{\text{classes}}} = \frac{2}{60} = \frac{1}{30}$$

Probability
of being on
Brainbusters

Would they pick names out of a hat? Would
we have to do a test? Do I need to revise? What
do I need to revise? Everything? Everything
in the whole wide world? How can I do that?
Systematically? Alphabetically? Starting at
A for aardvark and working my way through
everything?!! Everything in the whole wide world?!
How long do I have?

Revising
general
knowledge
is nearly
impossible.

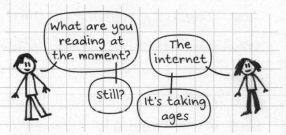

You'd have to read the whole Internet, which is
basically all the world's knowledge rolled into one
place. It would take **FOREVER**. Even on *Mastermind*
sometimes people who are really smart get loads
of answers right on their specialist round and then
only manage a few on the general knowledge
round – you just can't prepare for it. If I was on
Mastermind, my specialist subject would be capital
cities. I tried to learn a load once (I know – I must
have been really bored) and now I'm quite good at
them.

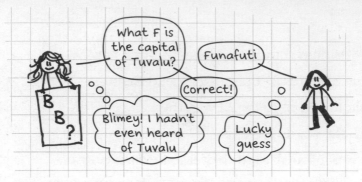

But me and Keziah are both good at general
knowledge. I reckon we're the brightest in the class
and we know weird stuff too, like the fact starfish
don't have brains. How crazy is that? How do they
even think? I guess starfish probably don't have
that much to think about, to be fair (a bit like Suzie
Ashby). But to not think at all?! They can't plan
their actions, so everything must be spur of the
moment, I guess.

Keziah told me once that male seahorses give
birth. Good on seahorses! I'd love to see human
men do that! Just imagine – my dad having a baby!

I wish men could have babies. Why should women do all the hard work?

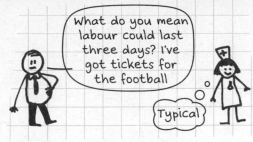

Last time I went round to Keziah's house, Mal (one of her dads) showed us it on YouTube (seahorses, that is, not my dad having a baby!). They literally shoot thousands of baby seahorses out of their tummy like they're coughing them up. It looks **SO** funny.

Just then, Mr Hastings, the deputy head, knocks on the classroom door and calls Mrs Mannan over. They talk for a while and everyone wonders what is going on or who is in trouble. We all murmur anxiously until Mr Hastings clears his throat and says in a firm voice, 'That's not a very Sparrowhawk attitude,' at which point we all hush up. What is going on? Have they got CCTV of Krantz and noticed me in it? Am I in trouble for not reporting it? Have they told my parents? Would I get a criminal record? Would I go to a young offenders, institution? Why

have I ruined my life so young?

'I'd like to introduce you all to Jake,' says Mr Hastings, 'and it would be wonderful if you could set him a good Sparrowhawk example. Thank you, Mrs Mannan, that will be all.' Then he leaves, although not before ushering a new kid into the classroom.

'Class, we have a new member,' says Mrs Mannan, standing to one side to reveal the new boy.

I look up to see a face I recognise but can't quite place. Browny-blond hair swept to one side as if he is in a boy band, backpack on his shoulder and both hands in his pockets with an air of casual confidence. And **BAM!** That's when it hits me. Jake is the boy who bought Bluey. Jake the cat burglar is my new classmate.

CHAPTER 6

The Empty Seat

I always thought a cat burglar was someone who steals cats but it turns out it isn't.

> *Oxford English Dictionary*
> *definition of cat burglar:*
> **cat burglar** cat bur.glar /ˈkat ˌbərglər/
> *noun* A burglar who enters a building by
> extraordinarily skilful feats of climbing.

Help! Someone put me in a sack and is taking me away!

Normal burglar (stealing a cat)

Someone has left the window open. I'll climb inside and take their TV!

cat burglar (stealing a TV)

I'm sure someone climbed past the window!

Don't be silly, dear!

Jake should be in Krantz's class, not mine; they'd get on like a house on fire. Or rather, a house being burgled.

So, Keziah is leaving and Jake is joining. Great.

Smug Jake who is now the proud owner of the cutest kitten in the world, which should belong to **ME**. Jake begins to tell the class a bit about himself. Nothing ground-breaking, mind you. He's just moved here to Ealing. Yes, Jake, we all live in Ealing, that's why we all go to this local school that's in Ealing. It would be dumb to move to Jamaica and go to school in Ealing.

He no longer has to share a bedroom. Bully for you, Jake, but **MORE** bully for whichever sibling had to put up with you droning on like this. Bet they're chuffed you have your own bedroom now.

50

Jake's brother

He ends his boring old speech with the 'fact'
that he owns the cutest kitten ever.
His name is Nigel and he's
six weeks old.

Thanks, Jake: rub it in
my face that you stole my
kitten, why don't you? When he mentions Bluey –
or should I say Nigel? No, I shouldn't – everyone
says 'aww!'. (Suzie and Alison awwwed a bit louder
than the rest of the class, of course.) As soon as
he finishes he gets a round of applause – started
off by Mrs Mannan, I should point out. A round
of applause? Really? It's not as though he's done

something
remarkable
or clever; he's
just said a few
sentences about
himself. Hardly applause-worthy.

Mrs Mannan thanks Jake (although for what, I don't know) and tells him he can sit down in the empty seat next to **MINE** . . . the seat that I am saving for Keziah! Unbelievable. I have to put a stop to this and fast.

'Uh,' I splutter, turning red. 'That seat's taken. It's, uh, Keziah's.'

'I don't think it is,' says Mrs Mannan.

'But, Mrs Mannan,' I protest, 'Keziah's flight has been rescheduled and I promised on my life that I would save her a seat next to me. She's back tomorrow, which means the seat is only free for the next few hours so really we'd all be better off by putting Jake in the other empty seat at the back of the class next to Axel.'

There is a short silence during which I think my plea has worked. But, no. Mrs Mannan does not take kindly to my well-reasoned arguments.

'That seat does not belong to anyone. Not you or Keziah. Nor does it belong to Jake or anyone else in this class . . .'

Yeah, OK, list the names of everyone in the world the seat doesn't belong to, why don't you?

. . . nor does it belong to Mickey Mouse or Daffy Duck or Donald or Uncle Scrooge for that matter, or William Shakespeare or the Royal Family or Thelma and Louise, nor . . . the Dalai Lama or the Brontë sisters or Mother Teresa or the President of the USA or the Pope or Madonna or Flipper or Harry Potter or Hermione, or Bart, Marge, Lisa, Maggie or Homer or Smithers, Apu, Mrs Krabappel or Skippy the Kangaroo. Nor does it belong to Romulus or Remus or the Mr Men or any Big Brother contestants or Ozwald Boateng. It doesn't belong to Pelé, nor the Pied Piper of Hamelin nor Bill Gates or any YouTubers or Ronald McDonald or the Prime Minister of Tuvalu or any world leader. This chair is not the property of Elsa or Anna or Kanye West, nor does Pac Man own it. Neither Super Mario, King Kong or Hillary Clinton possess this chair. Nor does it belong to Heston Blumenthal or Yoda, or any animals in the Makgadikgadi Pans National Park in Botswana, Buddha nor Ganesh, Shiva, Parvati or any gods or goddesses including God. Neither Kermit the Frog nor the Teenage Mutant Ninja Turtles or the Queen or Shania Twain. Not Father Christmas or his elves or Rudolph the red-nosed reindeer nor Engelbert Humperdinck or Gandhi or Julius Caesar or Henry VIII or any of his wives. Barry Scott does not own this chair, nor Mel, Kev or Bob. Nor do Alexandra Allden or Jenny Jacoby. The Grand Old Duke of York does not even own this chair. Understand?

'This seat belongs to the school and as their representative I will decide who sits in it and that will be Jake.'

Talk about long-winded. Worse still, she is now advocating my *death* because, as I pointed out already, I had promised on *my life* that I'd save Keziah a space next to me. To tell you the truth I hadn't (too risky), but I thought this little white lie might help my cause. It doesn't.

'But, Mrs Mannan, pleeaasse, if you value my life . . .'

Now that *really* annoys her. (To be fair it *is* pretty annoying, but it's fun annoying her. Me and Keziah used to do this thing where we would clap when she was looking at the blackboard and then she'd look up and we'd be doing jazz hands. Mega-annoying but **SOOOOOOOOOOOO** funny!!!)

She then threatens me with the green seats, as if dangling death over my head isn't enough! The green seats are the worst possible place you can ever end up at school. They're right outside the head teacher Mrs De Souza's office. You have to sit on them and wait until she calls you in. You have to do something **TERRIBLE** to get on the green seats. I have never been there before, but then again I'm pretty well-behaved really.

In the whole of last year we've only had three green-seat incidents in our class:

1. Finlay Riordan scratched Tayo Akinola's face and it started bleeding. Finlay said it was self-defence and that Tayo had tried to punch him. They had been arguing over whether Tayo had lied when he said his dad had met the whole of the England football squad. Tayo lies about everything. He once told us his dad got knighted and was Sir Akinola. Untrue. But amazingly, Tayo *had* told the truth this time. His dad had repaired an air-conditioning unit at the ground where they were training. He brought a photo in the next day to prove it.

2. Suzie Ashby and Alison Denbigh were caught painting rainbows on their nails in science. We're not allowed coloured nails at school, let alone permitted to paint them in class, so I'm not sure what they thought they were doing.

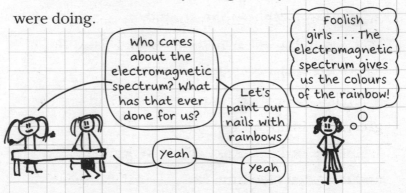

3. There was this angry, obnoxious boy called Liam Phipps who had quite a few incidents,

including one on his first day when he said a really rude word to the PE teacher Mr Edwards. I never found out for sure *which* rude word he used, but there were all sorts of rumours (and rude words) flying around. He was only in our school for one term. Sometimes I wonder whether he secretly got expelled.

I have never even had detention. I've been told off lots but mostly for low-level stuff like talking in class and messing around. I'm not about to get 'green-seated' because of some big-headed cat thief, so I keep quiet while Jake takes Keziah's seat next to me. Mrs Mannan says that I have to look after him for the day and show him around.

Look after him? What is he, a baby? Next she'll be asking me to change his nappies.

The rest of the day is just as annoying. Jake tries to make conversation with me, which I refuse to entertain.

He acts like nothing has happened. He is probably laughing at me behind my back the whole time, thinking, 'Ha ha, I've got her kitten!'

Just when I think he couldn't possibly irritate me any more, he manages *exactly that*, by putting his hand up in class to literally every question asked. It is like he is doing it just to get at me. So then I decide to put my hand up to every question too and before we know it we are in a question-answering war. Even Mrs Mannan is finding it a bit odd, and to make matters worse Jake is actually quite clever. We keep firing our hands into the air before she can finish her sentences and just as the score is drawn even, I get chosen to answer a question I have no idea about. I look really dumb.

Even dumber when she proceeds to ask him the answer and he gets it right.

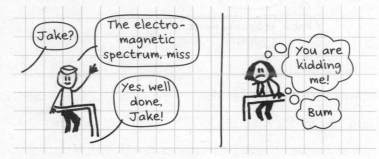

What sort of person knows what range of frequencies incorporates gamma rays at one end, long waves at the other with the colours of the rainbow somewhere in between? I've looked it up since.

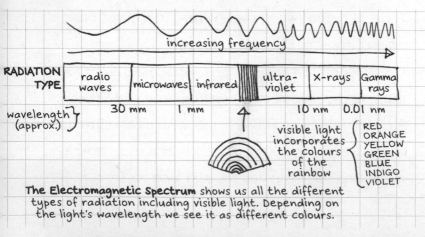

The Electromagnetic Spectrum shows us all the different types of radiation including visible light. Depending on the light's wavelength we see it as different colours.

After that I can't even catch up with him because she bans us both from answering.

By lunchtime I am so wound up, I almost feel like Liam Phipps . . . **VERY ANGRY**. Come to think of it, maybe he was just misunderstood.

I skulk off to the lunch hall with Jake still in tow, trying to be nice to me, while I ignore him. Take the hint, Jake! I can't be friends with a cat-snatcher. I even start being extra nice to everyone else who we pass to show him what a nice person I am . . . just not to him. I say hi to members of teaching staff, people in other year groups, the caretaker. Anyone and everyone.

I also make sure to have a lovely long conversation with Selina, my favourite dinner lady, during which I deliberately laugh lots in his eyeline, so he can see just what fun I am. After a while he seems to get the message and hangs back a bit. Then Alison Denbigh asks him about his kitten, but before he has a chance to speak Suzie Ashby starts blathering on about her millions of pets and, I gotta say to his credit, he doesn't act in the least bit interested!

I tell Selina everything. Selina must be, like, a hundred and three years old, but she acts like she's barely eighteen. She is outraged and promises to give him a smaller portion of chips than everyone else. **LOVE HER!** Later, when Jake sits down next to me with his tray, I grin sweetly and say, 'Enjoy your chips!' smirking

to myself as I shovel a load into my mouth from my chip mountain. He thanks me, a bit bemused. Nice one, Selina. It's good having friends in high places.

CHAPTER 7

Brainstorming

Lunchtime feels like it lasts three years because I can't wait to find out how the school will be picking the two Year Fivers to go on *Brainbusters*. It has to be a general knowledge quiz, surely? It can't be pulling names out of a hat, can it?

If they don't choose based on merit, they could end up with any old person going on the show who just happened to get picked, lucky-dip style.

And the two lucky contestants are Mickey Mouse and Donald Duck!

They might end up with Suzie Ashby and Alison Denbigh and their extremely limited general knowledge.

I know it seems like I'm really mean to them, but they aren't the brightest of people so sometimes can act pretty stupid. I don't like to bad-mouth people flippantly, so I'll back this up with some (of the millions of) examples of their thickness . . .

1. Suzie doesn't know what voting is. How can you not know what voting is? Our whole country is run on the outcome of voting. I mean, where was she all those times we voted for members of the school council, or did she just not listen to what we were doing? Mind-boggling.

2. Alison thinks you make tea by putting a teabag in a kettle. I know this cos Roubi was in the same year as one of her brothers who continually teases her about it.

3. Suzie thinks Topsy and Tim off the TV are real. Does she think it is a documentary or something?! I mean, really??!!

4. Alison thinks prawns are vegetables.

5. Neither of them can tie a bow properly.

All Suzie cares about is how she looks and everything she owns

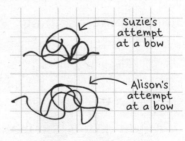

being glittery and perfect. She is the sort of person that would never get pen on her hands or spill her drink. I can't even imagine her blowing her nose. The worst thing about her, though, is that she is so BORING. Alison hangs on her every word and agrees with everything she says, which makes Suzie think she's ACTUALLY interesting! Alison is just like a smaller version of Suzie.

SPOT THE DIFFERENCE

Suzie Ashby   Alison Denbigh

Suzie is slightly taller
Alison has faint freckles
Suzie's shoes have bows
Alison's hair is slightly darker
Suzie's voice is more annoying
Alison's eyes have brown flecks

They go around with matching bags, and often have the same fancy stationery or pencil case or shoes. They probably wish they were twins. They both look down on people or things they don't think are cool enough to meet their very high standards. I certainly don't measure up. Alison is the sort of person who at lunchtime will sit next to you, plonk her tray down and just as you're about to tuck in to your food she'll look at it and say . . . 'Ugh, you're not gonna eat that, are you?'

Things I would like to say back . . .
1. 'No, I'm going to smear it all over your face, so I don't have to look at you.'
2. 'No, I just put it on my plate to annoy you.'

3. 'Eat it? No, I'm going to talk to it. I thought it would be capable of better conversation than you.'
4. 'Seriously?! An animal died so I could eat this meal. It probably lived next to a motorway and only ate grass its whole life, so show some respect.'

Things I actually say back . . .
1. 'I thought it looked quite nice.' *(Defensively)*
2. 'It's the vegetarian option. I don't eat pork, so I didn't want sausage and mash.' *(Apologetically)*
3. 'Ha ha, er . . . yeah.' *(Nervously)*
4. Nothing. I just shrug. *(Blankly)*

My mum is quite militant about us not 'disrespecting food'. I guess it's because my parents are from Bangladesh and they've seen first-hand lots of poor people who have to beg for money so they can eat. Whenever I say I don't want my food my mum always says: 'There are people who can't afford to eat.' Suzie's mum would probably say, 'Oh, sweetheart, don't you like pan-fried duck breast in an orange jus? Let me put it in the bin and get you something else. What would you like? Chocolate ice cream with caramel sauce, marshmallows and

sprinkles? Of course, my darling. Coming right up.'
My mum always makes us finish **EVERYTHING** on
our plates.

I nearly forgot . . . *Brainbusters*. I suddenly feel
sick. Why didn't I revise a few key things over
lunch? I'm so unprepared post-summer holidays;
my brain is in sieve mode. I guess we're all in the
same boat. I'm not usually too bad at tests, but only

if I know what
to swot up
on. And if it's
not the whole
internet,
obviously!

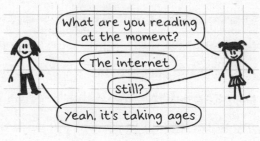

And what about Keziah? She'll have to sit the
test on Monday. Maybe I should offer to do mine
with her so she's not on her own and that way I
can revise over the weekend! Now *that* is a plan!

Maybe I can even
get someone who's
already done it to
drop me hints on

what will come up! Ha ha! Brilliant!

'Now, class,' says Mrs Mannan, 'after thinking
long and hard about how to choose contestants
for the *Brainbusters* TV quiz show, the school has
decided it will be the two winners of this year's Year
Five science competition.'

'WHAT?!?!'

I did *not* see that coming!

Our head and deputy head both have a science
background and LOVE promoting science in
school. We have science fairs, science days, science
clubs, science cups, all sorts. We even have our
own teacher just for science, Mrs Chen. The school
is science-**OBSESSED**. If there's any way they can
make our days more sciencey, they will . . .

The Year Five science project is always a big event. Everyone has to come up with a clever science project over one weekend. Two people win a prize (the prizes are always really good, like a microscope or telescope) and all the best entries are put on display in a mini exhibition in the main reception area. People really go to town on it and get mega-competitive with their entries.

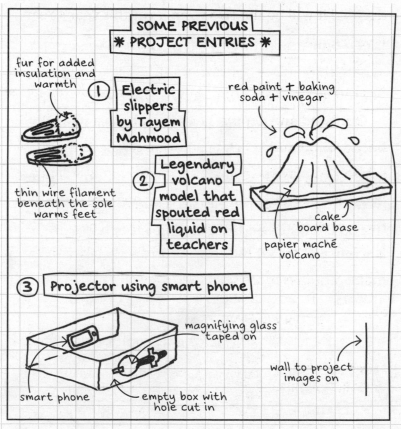

SOME PREVIOUS ✳ PROJECT ENTRIES ✳

fur for added insulation and warmth

① **Electric slippers by Tayem Mahmood**

thin wire filament beneath the sole warms feet

red paint + baking soda + vinegar

② **Legendary volcano model that spouted red liquid on teachers**

cake board base

papier maché volcano

③ **Projector using smart phone**

magnifying glass taped on

wall to project images on

smart phone

empty box with hole cut in

The competition is usually held towards the end of the first term, but Mrs Mannan explains that they have decided to bring it forward this year to fit in with the schedule of the TV show. Hmmm. I'm not sure how I feel about this . . .

I have to get on *Brainbusters*, though, so it doesn't matter how I feel. Time to come up with an **AWESOME** idea. And fast. I have sixty-four hours before Monday morning, minus thirty hours of sleep time (important to keep my brain focused). That's thirty-four hours in total, EST (Excluding Sleep Time).

So I am now looking at everything through 'science competition' eyes. Walking home from school and seeing cars go past, I'm thinking I could design a model of the electric car of the future. It could have a windscreen with a touchscreen

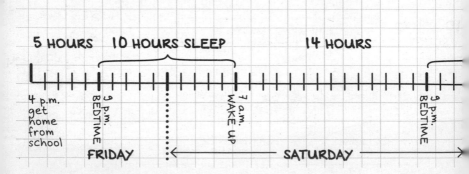

dashboard at the bottom. It would be eco-friendly, streamlined and aerodynamic so short flights would be possible too. There'd be loads of other little features as well, like a hot and cold drinks dispenser.

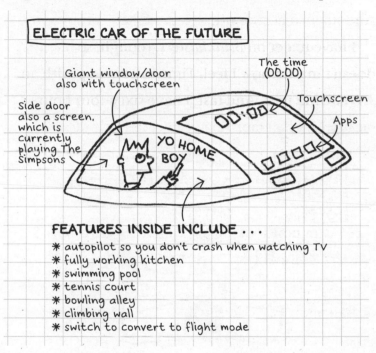

ELECTRIC CAR OF THE FUTURE

The time (00:00)

Giant window/door also with touchscreen

Side door also a screen, which is currently playing The Simpsons

Touchscreen

Apps

00:00

YO HOME BOY

FEATURES INSIDE INCLUDE . . .

* autopilot so you don't crash when watching TV
* fully working kitchen
* swimming pool
* tennis court
* bowling alley
* climbing wall
* switch to convert to flight mode

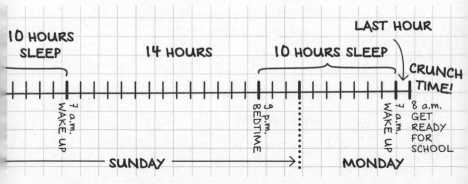

10 HOURS SLEEP

14 HOURS

10 HOURS SLEEP

LAST HOUR

CRUNCH TIME!

7 a.m. WAKE UP

9 p.m. BEDTIME

7 a.m. WAKE UP

8 a.m. GET READY FOR SCHOOL

SUNDAY

MONDAY

At dinner time, as I eat, I'm thinking I could do a cross-section of the human body that you put food in and watch its journey from food glob to poo. Maybe if I put brown paint in the lower abdomen, when the food gets pushed through, the results coming out of the bum would be authentic. I could use my old life-size baby doll and cut it in half and put rubber tubing inside to be the oesophagus and gut.

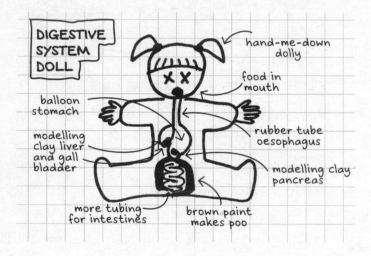

DIGESTIVE SYSTEM DOLL

hand-me-down dolly

food in mouth

balloon stomach

modelling clay liver and gall bladder

rubber tube oesophagus

modelling clay pancreas

more tubing for intestines

brown paint makes poo

Then in the bath that night, I'm thinking maybe I could come up with something to do with the water cycle . . . or actual cycling.

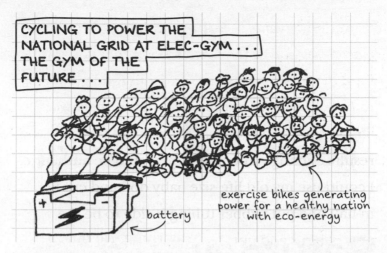

CYCLING TO POWER THE NATIONAL GRID AT ELEC-GYM... THE GYM OF THE FUTURE...

battery

exercise bikes generating power for a healthy nation with eco-energy

Argh! I just can't decide and I'm not happy with any of my ideas. I've wasted five of my thirty-four hours thinking and have come up with nothing.

I am still awake well past my bedtime. I go downstairs and declare I can't sleep and Dad says it is because everything is so bright due to the full moon. He shows me out of the window. The starry night sky looks awesome with the glowing circular moon acting as a massive centrepiece for all the delicate constellations surrounding it. Simply stunning.

Looking up, I suddenly know what my project will be – and I know it is a winning idea.

CHAPTER 8

Restraining Order

Saturday

morning. No time to lose. I'm going to make a scale model of the solar system. It will be beautiful and attention-grabbing, just like the real thing. Genius! I immediately get to work. First, I will make the planets. I narrow it down to three options . . . papier-mâché, fruit or cubes.

If I make the planets out of papier-mâché, then I will also be able to paint them, but it will be very hard to make them spherical. I always find papier-mâché ends up looking a bit messy, like scrunched-up, painted newspaper balls. A bit too 'nursery school'.

Class, who has dropped this rubbish?

Uh, that's Cookie's science project

Fruit has the advantage of already being round – but will it rot in the long run?

Maybe I'll varnish it. I could use a honeydew melon as the sun and round fruit, such as apples, oranges and tomatoes for the other planets. (Yes, a tomato is a fruit. Yawn, yawn. It has seeds, in case you didn't know, but everyone does know.)

If I go for cubes instead of balls, I could use square boxes and dice and stock cubes and all sorts of other cube-shaped things to make the planets. The sun could be the tissue box we have in the hallway. It would look neat but wouldn't be accurate. I may get marked down.

Fruit it is. I will call it 'The Fruit Solar System'. At breakfast I examine every fruit we have in the house. We don't have a honeydew melon (the sun), so I decide to use a yellow sponge ball from the garden instead. It looks a bit dirty, so I soak it in soapy water in the bathroom sink.

I then look up the sizes of all the planets and decide my model will NOT be to scale. That would be impossible anyway since the sun is 820,000 times bigger than Earth. A honeydew melon is not

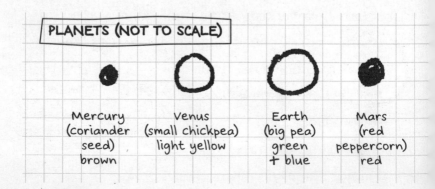

820,000 times
bigger than a pea.
My model will just
show the planets
in very rough size
order instead.

This is all turning out to be a lot more complicated than I first thought. Armed with a ruler, I go to the kitchen and begin measuring up.

Twenty-six hours left EST; I finally have all my planets. Unfortunately they aren't all fruit . . .

I decide to rename my project 'The Edible Solar System' and ask Mum to buy me a honeydew melon for the sun, but she says our new next-door neighbours are coming over for dinner later, which means . . .

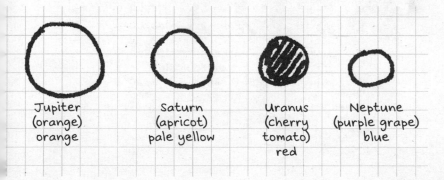

Jupiter
(orange)
orange

Saturn
(apricot)
pale yellow

Uranus
(cherry
tomato)
red

Neptune
(purple grape)
blue

a) She probably won't have time to get one, so I'll have to call it 'The Nearly Edible Solar System' and use the sponge ball.

b) Me and my sister will have to sit down at the dining table and help entertain. This will eat into my project time by at least a couple of hours.

Need to crack on . . .

Like the evolution of man, my project idea has gone through multiple stages.

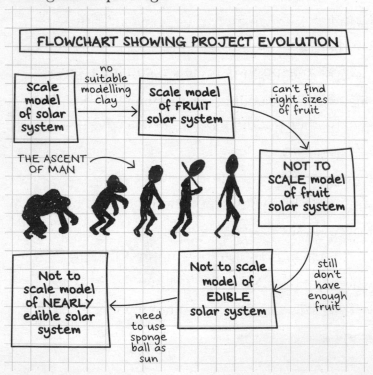

FLOWCHART SHOWING PROJECT EVOLUTION

Scale model of solar system

→ no suitable modelling clay →

Scale model of FRUIT solar system

can't find right sizes of fruit

THE ASCENT OF MAN

NOT TO SCALE model of fruit solar system

still don't have enough fruit

Not to scale model of EDIBLE solar system

need to use sponge ball as sun

Not to scale model of NEARLY edible solar system

The sponge ball still looks disgusting and dirty after washing, so as soon as I've eaten my lunch I go into the garden to see if we have any other suitable balls. Lo and behold, like a miracle, there she (he) is . . . Bluey. She (he) has found me. I can't help but call Bluey she instead of he, and I think she (he) likes it, so I'm going to continue. I would recognise Bluey anywhere. I scoop her (him) up in my arms, cuddling her (him) tightly.

I feel so happy. My project is coming together, *Brainbusters* is within reach, and I am sitting in my back garden cuddling Bluey, as though she were my very own pet. Life is good. Her soft fur feels luxurious on my cheek as I snuzzle her in the warm sun. Sheer bliss. Hang on, how did Bluey find me? How does she know where I live?

A voice interrupts my thoughts. 'Hey, Nigel, where are you? Nige – here, boy!'

Ugh. I'd recognise that annoying voice anywhere!

A head pokes round
from the passageway at
the side of the house.

Jake?!?!

You have got to
be kidding me!! He is now trespassing in my back
garden. What is this boy? Some kind of stalker?
At this rate I'll have to get a restraining order and
police protection.

At least that way he'd get moved to another
school and I could sit next to Keziah in our precious
last few months together!

Which reminds me, Keziah's flight will have landed
by now. I'll have to ring her and fill her in on
everything.

'Jake, what on earth are you doing in my
garden?!' I ask, horrified.

It turns out Bluey ran from his garden into ours through a gap in the fence.

Huh?

His garden?!

A gap in the fence?!

Hang on a second . . . **NO WAY!!**

Jake's garden is next to *our* garden?!

Jake is our new next-door neighbour?!!

Jake is coming round to dinner tonight?!!

!!!!NO WAY AGAIN!!!!

Before I can think straight I turn in a dramatic fashion and flee back into my house, leaving him there on his own, looking bewildered.

CHAPTER 9

The Nearly Edible Solar System

Now would be a good time to ring Keziah; she always cheers me up. We often laugh till our bellies hurt about private jokes that no one else even gets.

Keziah tells me all about her holiday and I tell her about Bluey, Krantz, Jake, and of course the *Brainbusters* science competition. Keziah doesn't want to do the science project, so we are gonna

pretend she doesn't get back until Sunday night!!
She can't think of anything worse than being on
TV! I'm not at all surprised. The thing is, Keziah
is a weird mix of confident, outgoing and funny,
while still being shy at the same time. She gets really
reserved in front of strangers, but is the complete
and utter opposite with people she knows.

After the Keziah catch-up, it was already
4.30 p.m. (nineteen and a half hours left EST).
Precious minutes are ticking away till Monday
morning.

I have less than three hours before dinner, so I dry
the sponge ball with a hairdryer. I come up with
the brilliant idea of painting it with orange and red
blotches to hide the dirtiest bits. It ends up looking

really good, very fiery and sunlike.

Then I draw up some plans to help me put it all together and look up some facts about each planet.

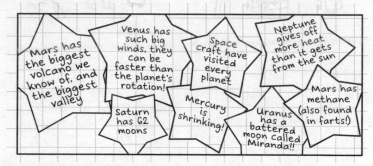

6.27 p.m. (seventeen hours and thirty-three minutes left EST) – I finish up for the night and make a last-minute attempt to get my parents to cancel Jake and his parents to no avail.

Jake is having dinner at ours . . . **NOOOOOOOO OOOOOOOOOOOOOOOOOOOOO!!!!!**

7 p.m. on the dot – Jake and his parents turn up with some posh chocolates and a bottle of wine. Mum thanks them for their gifts and tells them

we don't drink alcohol, which makes them all
apologetic and embarrassed. Tee-hee-hee!

'You must be Cookie,'
gushes Jake's mum. 'Jake's
told us all about you.'

Uh-oh, what did he
say? That he stole my
cat? That I didn't speak to
him for the whole of the

first day? That I made Selina give him fewer than
ten chips? That I stormed away from him in the
garden?

My mum tells me to get him a drink and that I
will be in charge of looking after him. Not again!
What is this? Am I his carer all of a sudden? What a
baby.

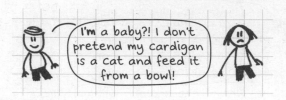

I don't plan on talking to him at all, so I'm not going to be much good at playing hostess.

Luckily his mum says he won't be staying to eat as they have a babysitter who is next door watching his brothers and sister. Babysitter – now that's what he actually needs. Why should I look

after him when really he needs a professional who's skilled at looking after BABIES?!

Jake's mum says she wanted Jake to meet my parents, seeing as we are both in the same class and it would be useful for sharing drop-offs and pick-ups like they had discussed. DISCUSSED?! Since when are they having secret discussions? I accidentally ask this out loud. Great. Now I look rude. Jake's mum told me they have only met once before, over the fence.

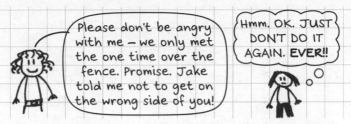

I really am going to need that restraining order if we're going to be together on the school run as well as having to sit next to each other in class. Thankfully he doesn't stay much longer and an awkward glass of orange juice later he is gone.

I cannot bear him. That whole encounter was SO awkward. Thank goodness he didn't actually stay for dinner.

His parents probably hate me as much as he does now. Good. Suits me.

Fifteen hours left EST – I wake up still reeling from all the Jake weirdness last night. At least I didn't have a swan dream.

Before Jake left he had sat in our kitchen sucking up orange juice through a straw and sucking up to my parents like the 'dream child', saying how much he loved the new school and its focus on science and how he wanted to do really well there. I could vomit.

Worse still, this was all *after* I had been rude in front of his parents. I could see my dad literally falling in love with him in front of my eyes.

My parents love
anyone studious.
They'll probably
be saying what a
bright, academic
boy he is at
breakfast. Spare me.

But instead, get this, my parents don't even
mention Jake; they are too busy telling me how
awful *his parents* were!! Amazing. Apparently they
couldn't stop showing off and bragging all evening.

My mum can't bear
them. Hurrah!
Looks like we won't
be on the school run
together after all.
Music to my ears.

'Ugh!' I look down at my project plans, which are
still on the kitchen counter. Jake has left a circular
stain on them with his glass of orange juice! This
boy just gets worse and worse, although it does
give me a good idea. I will stick my planets to a big
piece of paper and draw rings around them for the
orbits instead of suspending them with wire, as I

had originally planned. That would have been way too complicated. What was I thinking?! Get a grip, Cookie!! What next, rotating planets suspended on wires?!! This is a school project, not an exhibit in the Science Museum!!

Fourteen hours left EST – finish off my last piece of toast. I really don't like marmalade when the bits are too big. I don't want whole chunks of orange rind on my toast, thank you, just a few slivers is fine.

Twelve hours left EST – try using a glue stick, double-sided sticky tape and even staples to attach my sponge ball to the cardboard. None of them work so I stick the other planets on instead.

Eleven hours left EST – get peckish and look in the fridge. Why do my parents keep bread in the fridge? Everyone else's family has a bread bin.

Ten and a half hours left EST – try to sew the sponge ball onto my cardboard. It works! I am a genius! I am going to win this thing!

Nine hours left EST – lunchtime. We reheat food from Jake's parents' dinner. Why is it that sometimes food tastes so much better reheated the next day? Logic should dictate that food that is a day old should taste worse but actually it's the opposite. (My favourite day-old food is pizza.)

Eight hours left EST – find a pack of felt pens that have fallen down the back of the sofa. Amazing! I can draw all the orbits in different colours now! This project is going to look SO cool!

Seven hours left EST – there's a peeling bit of skin next to my fingernail. I hate it when that happens. I yank it off and now my finger hurts. Why does that happen?

Five hours left EST – stick on all my star facts. Looking good!

Four hours left EST – miracle brainwave! I decide to add in an asteroid belt between Mars and Jupiter using glue-stick and sugar.

Three and a half hours left EST – every time I move my solar system, half the sugar comes off. I'm hoping there's at least some asteroid belt left for the judging.

Three hours left EST – decide to label the planets while eating dinner to save time. This is down to the wire!

Two hours and fifty-six minutes left EST – a bit of ketchup lands on my project. Thinking quickly I relocate one of my star-facts to cover up the ketchup stain!

Two hours left EST – finished already! I am pretty pleased with the end results. Get me!

One and a half hours left EST – how good am I? Project done! I even have half an hour to spare before bed. I manage to catch the end of a programme about life in the Amazon. If I get on *Brainbusters* and a question about the Yanomami tribe comes up, I'll be laughing.

1: Sponge-ball sun
2: Mercury: coriander seed
3: Venus: chickpea
4: Earth: pea
5: Mars: red peppercorn
6: Jupiter: orange
7: Saturn: apricot
8: Uranus: cherry tomato
9: Neptune: grape

One hour left EST (for any last minute finishing touches tomorrow before school) – bedtime.

No swan dreams tonight! I can't wait for judging tomorrow. I really feel I have got this in the bag. I fall asleep smiling.

CHAPTER 10

Judgement Day

The next morning I belt my solar system into the car and make Mum drive really slowly over the speed bumps. This is extremely delicate cargo.

I am dying to get to

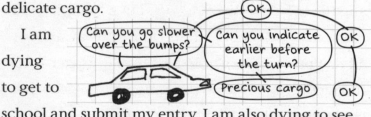

school and submit my entry. I am also dying to see Keziah. I've really missed her.

Keziah is on form!! It is SO good to see her. She looks especially healthy and glowing post-holiday!! So sad she is stuck at the back of the classroom next to Axel, while I'm next to Jake up front. We can't share our private jokes and have a laugh any more. Perhaps that was Mrs Mannan's plan all along.

Before assembly everyone takes their science projects and places them on the workbenches in the science lab. Most of them are covered up, so it is hard to assess the competition, but I feel quietly confident. I give Keziah a sneak peek and she **LOVES** it.

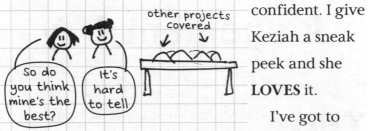

I've got to say, Neptune is looking a bit dodgy this morning. I had to pick the most spherical grape I could find and the only one that fitted the bill was already on the turn, so I'm hoping it isn't rotting away under all that paint and varnish. Meanwhile, Jupiter keeps threatening to come unstuck. Fingers crossed it all holds out till this afternoon's judging session. All in all, it's looking good, though. Before we left the house I even sprinkled glitter on the stars to give it more WOW factor. Wow! Wow! **WOW!! I CANNOT WAIT FOR THE JUDGING!!!**

After afternoon break it is judging time. There are some pretty elaborate creations, some quite involved diagrams, some weird inventions and a load of really ropey stuff.

Favourite bad entries ...

2 toilet rolls taped together

Binoculars – this is something you make in nursery, NOT year five. It has no scientific value! Just loo rolls!

fold-out stool legs

Strousers – a stool and trousers in one so you can sit down anywhere, without a chair. It'd never work! Weird!!

TV remote-control passer – so you don't have to get up to get the TV control! ... You'd still need to get up to get the truck control!! Duh ...

truck control

TV remote control tied to a remote-control truck

MRS MANNAN   MRS CHEN   MR HASTINGS

As Keziah doesn't have an entry, she stands next to me as I wait for the judges.

The judges are Mrs Mannan (not a fan of mine), Mrs Chen, the science teacher (inoffensive, smiley and placid), and Mr Hastings, the deputy head (strict some days, nice as pie on others, unpredictable).

Cookie, your project is leaking sugar ... HILARIOUS!

Cookie, your project is leaking sugar ... GREEN SEATS!

Good day   Bad day

They are walking round from entry to entry, each with a clipboard, making notes. I wish I could see what they are writing. I wonder if there are judging categories . . .

I am still quietly confident. So far the

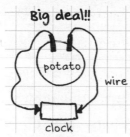

Big deal!!

potato

wire

clock

frontrunners seem to be Priti Prashad and Leo Mason. Priti has made a potato clock. *Pretty* basic. Anyone can stick two wires into a vegetable.

Leo Mason has made a working kaleidoscope. I have already seen the instructions for it on the internet. A piece of card, and a Pringles tube – essentially the

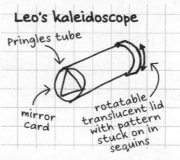

Leo's kaleidoscope

Pringles tube

mirror card

rotatable translucent lid with pattern stuck on in sequins

contents of our recycling bin. Way to go, Leo, and your amazing recycling bin that you use as a craft drawer!

Leo and Priti seem to be in with a chance because the judges compliment them both. I could happily do *Brainbusters* with Priti. She is in the other class but I know she is super-smart. Leo is also in the other class, but I've never really encountered him much. He's pretty shy and smells a bit funny, if I'm honest. Not a bad smell – just unusual. I quite like it. The way some people's houses smell a bit different.

Finally, after what feels like decades, the judges come over to me. Me! At last. I feel tense. I have butterflies in my stomach.

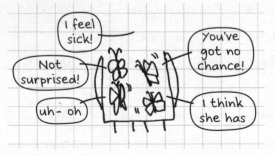

This is it: make or break time. The big moment I've been waiting for . . .

I pull the tea towel off my project with a flourish. I may have pulled a little too hard, as it dislodges Jupiter, which rolls to the other side of the classroom. Suddenly my model doesn't look half as good as I remember it. It just looks like bits of round food stuck on black cardboard.

Despite all this, Mr Hastings says it is 'original' and Mrs Chen says it is a 'real one-off'.

I still feel hopeful; these are great comments. Most people didn't get any comments at all.

Last up is Jake. Cat thief, chair-stealing Jake. I wonder what his rubbish offering will be like. He pulls the velvet covering off his project to reveal the most stunning model of the solar system **EVER**. It is made from modelling clay and copper wire, complete with suspended planets, all of which are **ROTATING** and **TO SCALE**. The whole thing is motorised and has a lit-up star cloth around the edges. There is a sharp intake of breath as everyone crowds around him in awe. It is delicate and beautiful. The teachers go gaga over him – like my dad did on Saturday night. I feel sick.

Unbelievable!!! We have done more or less the same thing. Well, kind of. What are the chances of that? Would they be able to give two solar systems a prize? Surely mine is more original? I don't see any fruit on his entry. My project is biodegradable!

Surely caring for the environment should be rewarded?

Perhaps *Brainbusters* is still within reach. Maybe I could even be team-mates with Jake. If I *have* to.

After the judging is complete everyone gathers round the front desk in the science lab to hear who the winners are. As I go over I catch Mrs Chen's eye and she gives me a **HUGE** grin. A sign? Once again I feel quietly confident.

Brainbusters, here I come!

Then Mrs De Souza arrives to announce the winners. I am bursting to hear my name. She begins with some chit-chat about how it's not the winning that's important, it's the taking part.

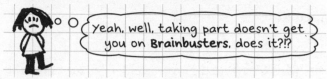

She goes on to say that the standard is very high
in this competition
and that it is
a shame there
can only be two
winners . . . the same old stuff she probably says
year in, year out.

 She then goes on
about what a privilege
it will be to represent
the school on TV
and how the school will be very proud to show
the world what great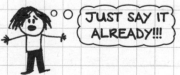
students it has blah
blah blah.

She clears her throat. I can hear my heart
thumping.

'Our first winner designed a wonderful
planetarium and obviously put a lot of time and
work into creating a truly superb model.'

Me, that's me!

'Jake Kay.'

That's not me. Ugh – **JAKE!!!!**

But Mrs Chen *had* given me a sign, so I could be next. I'm still in the running . . . They can't give a prize to one planetarium and not the other. I mean, we **LITERALLY** did the same thing.

'And his team-mate will be a girl who has truly excelled herself with a unique and almost biodegradable design made from food we can all find in our kitchen. The other winner is . . .'

Me! The other winner is me! I'm a girl! I used food from my kitchen! 'Unique' and 'original' are practically the same word!

'The potato clock!'

That's not me.

'Well done, Priti Prashad!'

That's not me.

CHAPTER 11

Why I'm No Longer Eating Circular Food

THERE IS NOTHING UNIQUE ABOUT A POTATO CLOCK.

Big deal – she decorated the potato with pictures of clocks through the ages (yawn) from sundials (bigger yawn) to grandfather clocks (ginormous yawn) to smartphones (infinite yawn x 1,000). But a winning entry? No way.

I want to scream. I feel hideous. Knocked for six. Like I've been punched in the gut. I'm *not* going on *Brainbusters* – the show I have followed so loyally ever since it began. I bet Jake and Priti don't even *watch* it.

I hardly ever miss it and even know some of the names on the credits, but I guess that counts for nothing. The floor assistant – whatever that is – is called Daisy Flowers. Funny name! I've always wondered if she has sisters called Lily and Rose! Bet Jake and Priti don't even know who Daisy Flowers IS.

(I have really gone off Priti. Priti Prashad? Pretty annoying more like.) Meanwhile, Mrs De Souza is still droning on . . .

'Highly commended this year is . . .'

Go on, describe an entry that could be mine and get my hopes up, then announce someone else's name.

'Leo Mason for his kaleidoscope.'

Fine – just break my heart immediately.

I can feel tears forming at the edges of my eyes and concentrate on holding them back. I busy myself rummaging around in my bag so no one else can see my blotchy face. What was Mrs Chen playing at, smiling at me like that? Giving me false hope. Toying with my emotions. I'm beginning to think the teaching staff at this school are all members of some sort of evil brotherhood.

Shoplifting Ms Krantz, lying Mrs Chen and grumpy Mrs Mannan, hell-bent on separating me and Keziah during her last term at school.

Thank goodness it is home time. I couldn't bear to go back to class and have to sit next to smug Jake after that.

How stupid, picking contestants for a general knowledge quiz from a science competition. That is SO dumb. Why not do a general knowledge test so you have the best candidates for the job?

Anybody's parents can help them with a science project and then, before you know it, thick people end up on *Brainbusters*. Jake could be thick. We hardly know the boy. Statistically speaking, he most likely is. There are way more thick people in the world than clever ones.

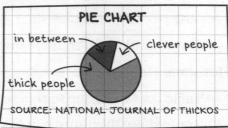

I feel so rubbish. I don't want face-to-face contact with anyone. Keziah offers to walk me home but human interaction would just make me burst into tears. I trudge home on my own instead, feeling totally sorry about my disaster of a life.

Of course my life isn't really a total disaster. I have a roof over my head, parents that feed me, my own bedroom . . . In the grand scheme of things I have it good. But right now I feel like things can't get any worse. Until they do. I get in feeling totally shattered, sink onto the sofa and switch on the TV for some escapism . . .

'Hello and welcome to this week's *Brainbusters*! The quiz show that puts you in your school's good books! Without further ado, let's meet those lucky contestants . . .'

NO, LET'S NOT!! We don't *even* know if they deserve to be there. For all we know they could have got onto the show by sticking a couple of wires into a raw potato.

coronation chicken sandwich

I defiantly switch off the TV, throw the remote control down, and flee to the kitchen to eat away my sorrows.

There, in the fruit bowl on the kitchen table, is a honeydew melon. I had asked my mum to get me one on Saturday. *Well, I don't want one NOW, do I?*

I don't need a stupid sun for the centre of my stupid solar system. In fact, I don't ever want any round food ever again in my whole life!! And that includes Maltesers. I must be in a bad way.

FIVE ROUND FOODS I WON'T MISS

CELERIAC – only had it once. Once was enough. Never heard of it before or since . . . PHEW!! UGLY VEGETABLE!!

GULAB JAMUN – Indian sweets that are fried milk balls soaked in honey or rose syrup. They make Christmas pud feel savoury! MEGA SWEET

RADISH – look red and appealing and as though tasty . . . do not be deceived. NOT TASTY!

CHRISTMAS PUDDING – always too sickly in my opinion. I do like raisins and soft fruit but thousands of them crammed together in every cubic centimetre . . . NO THANKS!! TOO SWEET!

MEATBALLS – better steeped in a tasty sauce. I always feel I'm not sure what's gone into them. Meat? What meat? Beef? Chicken? Kangaroo? Human? What if burgers were called meat burgers? . . . Not so tasty now, eh?!

I don't feel hungry right now anyway. Losing the science competition to

Mum, I don't want dessert. I'm on a diet.

Nonsense!

You should meet Jake – he'll put you off your food. You'll be skinny in no time!

Jake of all people is a major appetite-killer.

Mum and Dad can tell something is wrong with me. They keep asking if I am OK. I tell them I don't feel at all well, which is true. Mum says I look pale and takes my temperature.

I hold the thermometer up to my bedroom lamp when she isn't looking so it will show a high temperature. The old light-bulb trick.

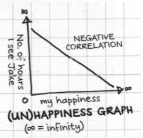

Works every time.

'If you don't feel better in the morning, you should probably stay off school,' says Mum.

Thoughts in my head: *I will NOT be feeling better in the morning and I will NOT be going to school. If I NEVER have to face Jake Kay again in my life it will be TOO SOON.*

'Ohhh, OK, Mum, maybe,' I say in my best ill voice, acting all disappointed.

I haven't told them that the science projects have already been judged and seeing how keen I had been to go to school this morning I think she believed my disappointment. The secret of faking illness in order to miss school is to pretend you love school at all other times.

At about 9 p.m. I realise I haven't eaten anything since lunchtime and that if I'm not careful I will waste away to nothing. Those evil teachers (and Jake) could then add manslaughter to their list of crimes. Mum, who can't stand the thought of not constantly feeding people, makes me come down to the kitchen for dinner.

That is when I see it and everything becomes clear.

The honeydew melon had distracted me from the real culprit behind my misery. Staring me in the face, there on the kitchen counter, were my solar system project plans . . . complete with orange-juice-glass ring stain on them. Jake's *orange-juice-glass ring stain.*

How did I not realise earlier?! Of course it wasn't a coincidence that our science projects were **EXACTLY** the same. Jake must have seen my plans when his parents came round for dinner and he **STOLE** the idea for himself. Not only has Jake stolen my cat, he's now stolen my project idea and, with it, my place on *Brainbusters.*

CHAPTER 12

Planets in the Pond

I had a scary swan dream last night. I haven't had one of those in ages. It was **SO** horrible. We were all in the science lab, but it was also my kitchen (the way weird stuff like that happens in dreams). Everyone's projects were being judged and then it was my turn. Only I didn't have a project so I opened the fridge and pulled out a honeydew melon and said it was the sun. Next, I ran to the fruit bowl and got a banana and said it was a crescent moon. After that I got all sorts of stuff like stock cubes for meteorites and cutlery for satellites and so on.

Everyone was laughing at me and the more they laughed,

This is my project — it's very original. I hope you like it. If you get peckish you can eat it!

the more stuff I pulled out from cupboards in desperation.

The judges, who were also my parents, called the head teacher in to announce the winners. That's when the door opened and this swan came in and started chasing me around the room, trying to peck my hand.

And then I wake up.

My mum pops her head round my bedroom door, takes one look at me, all sweaty and disturbed, and tells me I am staying off school.

'But, Mum,' I protest in an even more convincing ill person's voice than yesterday.

'No buts . . .' she says.

'OK,' I croak.

Easy. I didn't even need the light-bulb trick this time.

The funny thing about being unwell is that more often than not it doesn't affect your voice, but if you speak to anyone, especially on the phone, you feel the need to put on an 'ill' voice so they believe you, even if you genuinely *are* in a bad way.

I spend the whole day at home feeling miserable and extremely sorry for myself. Will I **EVER** be happy again? After eating some dry toast for breakfast, I lie on the sofa under a blanket watching daytime TV.

There is a phone-in with a doctor who says to one caller that extreme sadness, stress or depression can often bring on real illnesses. Uh-oh, I am at risk. I will need to take care of myself now. After that programme there is . . . guess what? A quiz show. Just my luck. I can't bear to watch.

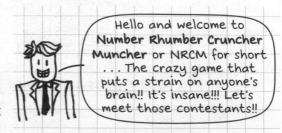

I switch off the TV and curl up into a ball. I must be tired from my restless night of bad swan dreams, because I doze off for a couple of hours. When I wake up Mum makes me some soup and sandwiches, which I guzzle down and gobble up.

Dad offers to take me to the pet shop later if I am feeling a bit better. I tell him I will **NEVER** go to the pet shop again. Mum suggests I get some fresh air, so I go out into the garden and am greeted by none other than Bluey. If only I could kidnap her (him) and run away . . .

I cuddle **her** tight and feel a little bit happier.

That evening Keziah calls to see if I am OK and to let me know she's got me copies of the work I missed at school. I tell her everything: how awful I still feel about *Brainbusters*, how Jake stole my project idea, as well as my cat, and how I did the light-bulb trick to get the day off school. She can tell how upset I am and really feels for me. She asks if I'll be back tomorrow. I tell her I'll probably take the rest of the week off and would really appreciate her getting me any other work I miss. Thank goodness for Keziah. I'll have a lot to catch up on . . .

'Oh yeah?' says an unimpressed voice. 'I think you've got some explaining to do.'

Dad has overheard my whole conversation with Keziah and makes it quite clear I will be back at school first thing tomorrow morning. Kick me when I'm down, why don't you? I am fuming. How dare he eavesdrop on my private conversation!

'Is there no such thing as privacy in this house?' I yell, storming off to the bathroom. The bathroom?! I do a U-turn and storm back past him into my bedroom. I hate it when I storm the wrong way.

At that moment the doorbell rings and next thing I know I hear Jake's voice from downstairs. Jake?! **YOU HAVE GOT TO BE KIDDING ME!**

He's brought me copies of the work I missed at school. **GO AWAY, JAKE!** Mum calls me to come downstairs. **RESTRAINING ORDER!** I turn the light off and pretend to be asleep, even though it is only 7.30 p.m. I can hear him laughing with my mum. **GROSS AND ANNOYING! UGH!**

Eventually he leaves. Thank goodness. **LEAVE ME ALONE, JAKE!** You've done enough damage already.

The next day at school I manage to avoid Jake quite successfully.

In geography we do a lot of fieldwork, so we are in the school's nature garden with clipboards. Nature garden?!! It's basically just a wild, fenced-off mess of an area that the school doesn't have to bother looking after! It's overgrown and unkempt and round the back of the playground, out of the way, where it's not too much of an eyesore.

In PE we do athletics (non-contact sports – good for Jake avoidance).

In food technology we make American-style pancakes using only a mug to measure out the ingredients.

All of this means the amount of time I am actually sitting down in the classroom next to Jake is minimal. It is surprisingly easy to get by without

having to speak to him. Just as well, because the thought of me not being on *Brainbusters* is still really painful and *he* is a constant reminder of it.

At lunchtime Selina suggests to me and Keziah that she could slip some poison in his food between now and *Brainbusters*! Selina is absolutely bonkers. It's the kind of thing I could actually imagine her doing.

Selina has a million grandchildren and at least as many stories about them. She once told me one of her grandchildren ate some soap and he was sick

the whole of the next
day. Maybe we could get
Jake to eat some soap?!!

After school Dad picks me up. He is acting all
weird. When I get in I run straight to my room,
and he calls up to me to come out into the garden.
Reluctantly I trudge down the stairs and outside.

He's bending over the pond, probably fishing out
a sweet wrapper or some rubbish that has blown in.
When I say pond, it's more the size of a puddle and
made of plastic that's pretending to be rock. It's not
very big, about the size of a small suitcase. I had
wanted a pond for ages, ideally one with a fountain.
Then, in Year Two, after a brilliant school report,
we got one (minus the fountain). Sometimes it gets
tadpoles, which turn into cute baby frogs.

'Come and see what's inside,' says Dad.

What?
Another
sweet
wrapper?

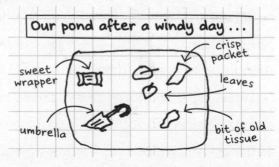

Our pond after a windy day . . .

I go over and peer in, only to see seven cute little multicoloured goldfish swimming about happily.

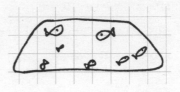

'They're yours,' says Dad, smiling.

I am so happy in this moment I could burst. Dad says they are my prize because he thinks I should have won the science competition, since I'd worked really hard and didn't even get any help on it. He tells me Jake's dad is an engineer and probably did his project for him, then adds that he hopes they aren't listening over the fence. We laugh. I say I hope they are. We laugh some more.

The science project was worth it just for these seven beauties. I decide to name them Mercury, Venus, Mars, Jupiter, Saturn, Neptune and Pluto. (I thought 'Earth' sounded too hippy-ish and a fish called 'Uranus' might get bullied by the others so substituted it with 'Pluto' even though it's no longer classed as a proper planet. But hey, I don't discriminate against dwarf planets.) Lucky me. Even Suzie Ashby doesn't have *seven* pets!

CHAPTER 13

The Cold Shoulder War

For the next week I continue to give Jake the cold shoulder. At first he persists with trying to break me, but when I get something into my head I have steely resolve, and I had got it into my head that this thieving boy is **BAD NEWS**. The more I give him the silent treatment, the more annoying he becomes. He keeps pulling stunts like when he brought my catch-up work over when I was off school. He'll offer me a snack if he is having one at break or save me a place in the dinner line and call me over, so that I look rude ignoring him.

I'm sure it is all for the benefit of other people, to 'prove' to everybody how nice he is and how mean I am. The more he does it, the more it annoys me. Thankfully, after a few days, he gives up. That's when we begin to get ultra-competitive again. Not just over who can answer questions first in class . . . but about **EVERYTHING**.

1. Who can finish work first?
2. Who can exit the door first?
3. Who looks like they're having more fun?
4. Who can get in the lunch queue first?
5. Who can eat lunch the quickest?

And so on.

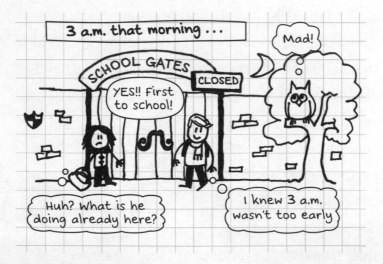

Meanwhile, Keziah and Axel are sitting next to each other and seem to be hitting it off big time. He actually doesn't look at the floor when he speaks to her. Wonders never cease.

Keziah seems to get on with everyone. She's so easy-going. I can't help but feel a little bit jealous when she has fun with people who aren't me, even Axel! I know it's wrong. My mum says jealousy is such an ugly personality trait. People should just be happy for each other, especially people they like. I should be happy Keziah is sitting next to someone who doesn't steal cats or project ideas. I'm not one of those friends who would say 'You look nice in that top' if she wore a totally gross outfit that made her look like a freak. I would tell her.

I want my friends to be happy and do well. Who would want their friends to be sad losers? Only mean people.

So why am I secretly annoyed that she thinks Axel is actually a nice guy? It all boils down to Jake. Yet again. The root of all my problems. The thing is, I want to sit next to a decent human being. Not one I'm having the Cold Shoulder War with.

TABLE

Cold War (1947-1991)	Cold Shoulder War (now)
US vs Russia	Cookie vs Jake
No direct fighting but the hatred is there	No direct fighting but the hatred is there

So, apparently, in science last week, Mrs Chen said that we'd be doing acid and alkali experiments outdoors. Outdoors! That means things could get messy.

Tina Mories and Clare Kelly ask whether we can do the volcano experiment. Mrs Chen says that one actually *is* an acid/alkali experiment, so whyever not?! Hurrah!! Mrs Chen is so meek and mild; she will usually go along with most things. She's such a soft touch.

PUSHOVER

Mrs Chen, can we do a nuclear explosion in class next week?

Well, I don't see why not . . .

The volcano experiment is a science project favourite. If you add lemonade, which is an acid, to baking soda, which is alkaline, in the right amounts you get neutral results – neither acid nor alkali.

But what's really cool is that the resultant mixture gives off carbon dioxide gas and the whole thing bubbles and foams, shooting upwards like a volcano.

Everyone is buzzing as we make our way outside in our white lab coats and protective glasses. It feels like we mean business. We have to pair up with our class partners, which means I am partnered with you-know-who. I'd been hoping to pair up with Keziah, but I seem to be doomed to spend the rest of my life with Jake.

There are all sorts of acids and alkalis.

We have to pick two experiments from a worksheet and then, once everyone has done them, we are all allowed to do the volcano experiment. Yay! Because Jake and I are both in 'silent but super-competitive mode', we finish ours really quickly. I feel all gloaty and pleased with myself because one of my experiments gives a really good result. I decide this needs praise, so make sure I catch Mrs Chen's eye.

'Lovely, Cookie,' she says as Jake looks on with envy. Jealousy. Such an ugly trait.

Result! I can almost forgive her misleading science-competition smile. (But not quite.)

I shoot her a big nauseating grin. 'Thanks, Mrs Chen.'

'Oh, Cookie,' she adds, 'we're running low on baking soda. While we wait for everyone else to catch up, can you nip to the kitchens and borrow a tub?'

I can tell Jake is annoyed that he hasn't been asked to run this errand. That boy's got serious jealousy issues.

Meanwhile, he has to put J-cloths on everyone's work stations instead so they can clean up after themselves! HA!

I go to the kitchens, find Selina and quickly bring her up to speed on all my goings-on. She chuckles and says she is still working on how we get me on *Brainbusters*. Short of leaving school and joining a new one, I don't see how this will ever happen.

She goes off and brings back a catering-

sized tub of baking soda. In moments from now, everyone will be trying to get the highest baking-soda fountain and I have the supplies right here in my hands. Maybe I can secretly offload a bit into my pocket and slip it in when no one is looking?

Mrs Chen will definitely ration it out. I tell Selina that my fountain HAS to outdo Jake's. She flashes me a smile and announces she has just the thing, then disappears for a few minutes, eventually returning with her handbag. Grinning mischievously, she pulls out half a packet of Mentos. If you have ever looked up Mentos and lemonade on the internet, you'll know that this dastardly combination creates a super-high lemonade fountain that shoots up for metres and metres.

I give Selina a huge hug, slip the Mentos into my pocket and rush back to the lesson, baking soda in hand.

We all have to choose an empty plastic bottle for our fountains. By the time I get back everyone has chosen the best ones. Jake has picked the biggest. Obviously. He'll be able to pour more lemonade in than me. MORE lemonade to react, giving off MORE carbon dioxide and making MORE lemonade fountain.

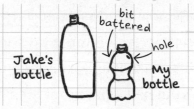

SO selfish! This is war. I will use more than one Mento if I have to. As I predicted Mrs Chen only gives us a tiny amount of baking soda each. We both tip our baking soda into our bottles. Jake's fountain shoots up high into the air. And mine? Nothing. So, when no one is looking, I slip a Mento in . . .

Nothing. Maybe it's got stuck in the bottle neck? I quickly slip another one in. Still nothing.

So then I tip ALL the remaining Mentos in. *Still nothing.* But then . . .

BOOOOO OOOOOOOOO OOOMMMMM!!!

My fountain explodes like crazy. The bottle must have a small split near the top, which the lemonade also shoots out of, spraying me right in the face, covering my goggles so I can't see . . .

. . . which means I don't see the force of the explosion tip my whole bottle over, totally soaking Jake.

Jake must think I did this on purpose, because the next thing I know, he's tipping lemonade all over me.

I am drenched. Soaked right through to my underwear and completely sticky. Totally raging. Before I know what I am doing, I pick up a sodden, dripping J-cloth from our trestle table and fling it at Jake, who quickly ducks out of the way so that it

misses him – and hits Mrs Chen **SLAP BANG IN THE FACE**. Uh-oh.

Meanwhile, my bottle has rolled onto the floor and is spinning around like a lunatic stray firework, tripping me up in the process. I go flying and fall

right on top of Jake, knocking us both down onto the lemonade-drenched tarmac.

It is only then that the last of the lemonade stops spraying. Carnage. Everyone in the playground is in a state of complete and utter shock. I feel sick to my stomach. This is an expellable offence.

CHAPTER 14

The Green Seats

I have never seen Mrs Chen angry before. She's always smiley, calm and placid. She's really inoffensive apart from when she gave me false hope during the science competition judging. The sort of person who wouldn't say boo to a goose. (I don't really get that phrase. To be honest, I wouldn't say boo to a goose either. It might attack me. Hope I don't start having scary goose dreams now.)

People get away with murder in Mrs Chen's classes: late homework, chatting, sucking sweets, playing *Pokémon Go* . . .

But not, it would seem, soaking her with lemonade.

It is as if something within her has been triggered. This seemingly harmless little lady has grown monstrous and turned red with rage, erupting like the lemonade fountain before her. I can actually see the blood rise from her toes, up her body through her neck to her face and then her brain.

'COOKIE HAQUE AND JAKE KAY!!! GREEN SEATS NOW!!!'

THE METAMORPHOSIS OF MRS CHEN

I didn't know she had it in her. Her voice is usually so meek and mild, apologetic even. I was almost impressed.

Hello, class. It's science, sorry, I hope you don't mind ... Sorry for speaking but I have to teach you ... er ... sorry

Both Jake and I (and probably the rest of the class for that matter) are stunned by this metamorphosis. This new Mrs Chen is **REALLY SCARY**. Who would have thought it?

BOO!!!

She's scary! I'm off!

COME BACK!

We both turn white with fear (which is saying something, as I'm usually brown). We just stand there dumbfounded. Glued to the spot.

'NOW!!!!' she repeats as we try to mobilise into 'action' mode, still stuck to the spot in 'gobsmacked' mode. We finally scarper off as quickly as we can. It is as though we are in one of those *Tom and Jerry* cartoons where their legs start moving on the spot before *they* actually start running.

I'm stuck, can't move

Me too!

GREEN SEATS **NOW!!**

The soles of our shoes are sticky so we squelch
as we walk in silence along the corridors,
heads hanging low, feeling sorry for ourselves
and thoroughly ashamed. The walk from the
playground to the head teacher's office feels like it
lasts forever.

PLEEEEASEE can I see as few people as possible?
I think as I trudge to the green seats. The children
we pass en route give us mixed responses, ranging
from amusement to downright pity.

We pass Ms Krantz who looks at us, bemused.
I half shrug at her and think, *Who are you to judge?*
I know about the marshmallows, Krantz.

I have been thinking about this for a while.
Maybe it is my responsibility as a good citizen to

hand her in to the
relevant authorities.
Surely it is dangerous
for us to have a
criminal in our
midst, especially in

a school where safeguarding is a very important issue. Maybe I could use this opportunity in the head teacher's office to distract attention from my own crime (if you can call lemonade and Mentos a crime) to reveal to Mrs De Souza what her teaching staff are really like. Maybe instead of getting told off I'll in fact get rewarded now. I'll have to play it by ear . . .

As we sit in the green seats the lemonade begins to dry and my clothes become a weird combination of crunchy and sticky. I feel gross. Jake is sitting next to me in a silent fury.

This is hardly *all* my fault. OK, so I made my fountain go a bit higher with a little extra help. How was I supposed to know my rubbish bottle with a hole in it would tip over? I didn't do it on purpose. *He* was the one who threw lemonade over *me* and I couldn't see to defend myself. Mrs Chen got hit because *he* ducked. This is all HIS fault. **EVERYTHING IS ALWAYS HIS FAULT.** Things were good before he pitched up. Keziah sat next to me. Bluey was still in the pet shop. *Brainbusters* was there for the taking. Happy memories. How I yearn to be back in those heady times.

As it is quite a warm day we are drying out pretty quickly. Maybe we could try some damage limitation. If I tie all my hair back, it won't look as wet. After thinking it over carefully, I finally break my week-long silence with Jake. I suggest we take off our lemonade-soaked lab coats and leave them outside Mrs De Souza's office. Our uniform underneath doesn't look nearly as wet, as it is dark in colour. It is worth a shot. Jake looks at me as if I am deranged.

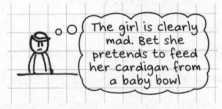

We probably only wait half an hour or so but it feels like the best part of a year. 'Cookie Haque and Jake Kay, Mrs De Souza will see you now.'

I have never been in the head teacher's office before. I had always thought I would be in here someday, but had never envisaged it quite like this.

I had always imagined it would be because I
was collecting a prize for my outstanding work or
because I had been appointed head girl. Maybe
even just for Mrs De Souza to say congratulations to
me as I had done so well on *Brainbusters*.

But no. None of the above. I am here because of
Jake.

'Take a seat,' says Mrs De Souza sternly. 'Would
one of you like to tell me what happened?'

What a dumb question! Obviously neither of
us would *like* to tell her what happened. We're not
stupid. We didn't *want* to be in trouble. We are
gonna keep schtum, not incriminate ourselves!

We both sit in silence, waiting for the other to pipe up. It is as if we have a new-found camaraderie because neither of us wants to speak up and get expelled.

Who would break the silence? Maybe now is a good time to mention Ms Krantz's kleptomania. I'm a big fan of long words and I'm a big fan of manias. **My top three manias are . . .**

1. Kleptomania – an obsessive love of stealing. I can see that people might get a buzz from taking things but stealing is wrong. I did once pinch a cola bottle from the pick 'n' mix and I must admit it was the sweetest-tasting cola bottle I've ever had. But the guilt was too much. I will never steal again.

2. Pyromania – an obsessive love of setting things on fire. I love watching fire, the way it sparks and dances around, but the thought of setting anything on fire myself is far too terrifying. I wouldn't even dare strike a match.

3. Clinomania – an obsessive desire to remain in bed. I think I may have this. I love being in bed and I love sleeping too! If I could just stay in bed some days I would. Shame my parents won't let me have a

TV in my bedroom.

Anyway, just as I am about to throw Krantz
under the bus, Mrs De Souza clears her throat.

'Well, Jake, it's only a matter of weeks before you
go on *Brainbusters*. I'm not sure you are the kind of
pupil we want representing our school.'

Jake turns white. Well, whiter. He wasn't brown
like me.

Oh no! She can't ban him from going on
Brainbusters, can she? That'd be awful and SO
unfair. It would all be my fault. I'd feel so guilty. I
can't stand by and let this happen. I'd rather he was
on it than Suzie Ashby or someone picked randomly
to replace him. At least he's a *bit* clever and
knowledgeable. I felt terrible when I wasn't chosen,
but at least I didn't have it snatched away from me.
I never *had* it in the first place. Besides, they'd never
let *me* replace him, so it would
just be a waste if neither of us
did it. What am I thinking . . . ?
I'm acting as if we're a team! I
suppose we kind of are at the
moment . . . Team 'Let's Not Get
Expelled'.

Own up?

No way. We're a
team. We even
share thought
bubbles!

Before my heart and mind have a chance to agree on what course of action to take next, my mouth bursts open and blurts the whole thing out. The kitten theft, the science project theft, the Cold Shoulder War, the competitiveness, Mum not liking pigeons, my bossy sisters, Keziah leaving, me not having Instagram, my bobbly jogging bottoms, Solihull being voted the best place to live in the UK, crazy swan dreams, wanting to win the science competition but always losing everything, including the egg-and-spoon race, Mrs Chen smiling at me and, finally . . . the lemonade fountain. It all spills out in one go, a bit like I was throwing up, except I was vomiting words instead of sick. I finish by saying that it wouldn't be fair if Jake didn't go on *Brainbusters* because

of what *I* did. Then, rather dramatically, and surprising even myself, I say, 'Punish me, not him!'

I'm not sure where any of that came from. Jake looks up, taken aback. As does Mrs De Souza. To be fair I was pretty shocked myself. It had just come out of my mouth from nowhere. I don't *actually* want to be punished instead of him.

Mrs De Souza pauses, taking everything in. I am certain I am about to get expelled.

Then she turns to me and, to my amazement, almost looks sympathetic. Jake doesn't look as smug as usual either, peering out from under his 'swept to one side' boy-band hairstyle. Wonders never cease. I think they both feel a bit sorry for me. Phew. Maybe I *could* stay at this school after all.

Knowing Mrs De Souza isn't angry is a massive release. I am kind of clearing it all out of my system like I am in therapy or something. A huge weight has been lifted off my shoulders. I want to laugh and cry at the same time.

I don't think Mrs De Souza has quite understood every detail of my story . . . the cat bit, the project theft – it was all a little garbled to be honest – but it doesn't really matter. I think she is actually impressed with my honesty.

Hang on, let me get to grips with this. There was a cat . . . sorry . . . er, where does **Brainbusters** come in? And an orange-juice stain? And why did you feed your cardigan from a bowl?

Never mind, who cares? The girl is honest. She can stay

In fact, she says Mrs Mannan had already mentioned to her that there has been some tension between the two of us since the beginning of term. She says it is a shame for us to be so silly as we are both such bright, exemplary students. And so our punishment would be to shake hands, make up and try to get along! **FOR REAL? UNBELIEVEABLE!**

What, no expulsion?

Good, we don't need to share thought bubbles any more

I put my hand out towards Jake and he reaches out too. It is as easy as that. We shake hands and declare a truce. The Cold Shoulder War is over and neither side has won. (Just like the real Cold War, I guess.)

CHAPTER 15

Bluey Has Green Eyes

We may not have been punished by the head teacher, but Mrs Chen is certainly not gonna let us off the hook *that* easily. As we are leaving her office Mrs De Souza tells us to change into our PE kit before we go back to class.

And so we do. Wearing clean, dry clothes again feels like luxury.

Mrs Chen must be quite jealous. She is still in her flowery silk blouse and although it must feel damp, sticky and horrible, the elaborate pattern disguises all the lemonade patches, so at least she doesn't look a state.

Everyone is indoors now, writing up their experiments, so Jake and I sit down in our places.

'*Who* told *you* to sit down? And *who* told *you* to get changed?' asks Mrs Chen, obviously still furious with us.

We reply that Mrs De Souza did, which she doesn't like at all, even though it is the truth. She acts as though we have answered back or acted cocky or something, and informs us that we haven't served our punishment yet. Served? What is this? A prison sentence or a telling-off over a bit of spilt drink on the floor?

She orders us to go to the library and write up our experiments in silence. After we finish that, we are to wash up **EVERYTHING** from the outdoor experiments and we aren't allowed to go home

until we have
finished . . . no
matter how late
it is!!! Come on!

It was a just a bit of spilt lemonade!

Usually we all tidy
our own stuff after
class experiments. She
has obviously told
everyone they needn't
bother and has saved
it all up for us on
purpose. Charming.

On our way to the library we bump into Ms
Krantz who seems to know everything. She says
a slightly damp Mrs Chen told her when she was
coming in from the playground.

She then adds, 'You two should know better!'

What? Are
you *actually*
kidding me?!
A lecture from
you? A common
criminal!

Looking back, it wasn't a lecture at all, just a light-hearted, teasing comment. But, yet again, before I know what my brain and mouth are doing, they gang up on me and blurt out loud, 'How can *you* say that to *us*? I know you stole those marshmallows, Mssssssssss Krantz.'

Jake goes white. Again. Why did I just say that? I try to backtrack and get out of it, and start speaking at a million miles an hour.

'Don't worry, your secret's safe with me. I don't even know why I mentioned it. It just came out. I didn't mean it. I won't tell anyone else. I'm not a snitch. I once stole a cola bottle from the pick 'n' mix. I'm just like you, really. Can we forget I said anything?'

She has absolutely no idea what I am talking about and makes me explain it to her, even though I just want to drop the whole thing. She listens as I recount the marshmallow Flump incident and then looks as though the penny has dropped.

She tells me that, in fact, she had already paid for the bucket of marshmallow Flumps, but when putting all her shopping in the boot of her car she noticed that the bucket had a broken seal, so took it back into the shop and showed the security guard, who told her to go and get a new one. So *that's* what I had seen her doing! Fair enough. If the seal was broken, there could have been a few Flumps missing or someone could have even slipped poison into it. No one wants a broken seal.

Phew! Thieving Krantz is just Krantz after all. Well, Ms Krantz. She can be my favourite teacher again. I can't wait to tell Keziah. She'll be so relieved. We both have a soft spot for Ms 'I am innocent' Krantz. I apologise to her, but luckily she finds the whole thing highly amusing and doesn't mind at all. (Thank you, Ms Krantz, you've always been my favourite.)

Writing up the experiment in the library doesn't take long at all. After we are done Jake and I head to the science lab to do the washing-up. Since our split-second handshake, we haven't really said much to each other, but now that we are washing up the sticky empty plastic bottles, we have a moment to reflect on everything.

'Can I ask you a question?' says Jake.

'I guess,' I reply.

'Why did you call me a cat burglar in Mrs De Souza's office?'

'Umm . . . Bluey . . . I mean, Nigel. She, er, he, was my cat first.'

I tell him how I had visited the pet shop every few days since Bluey was born.

The conversation that follows is revelatory . . .

1. It turns out Jake hadn't even *seen* me in the pet shop the day he got Bluey. He had no idea he had stolen my cat. He thought the first time we met was at school.

2. It turns out that Bluey IS a she! I never thought to check but it was Jake who got it wrong in the pet shop – not me! He was intent on having a cat called Nigel and he just assumed Bluey was a boy like I had assumed she was a girl!

3. Bluey has green eyes. Jake asks me why I call Nigel 'Bluey' and I say, 'Duh! Because of her beautiful blue eyes. Obviously.' I mean, it isn't rocket science. Plus, Bluey is a much better name than Nigel. Jake reveals his grandpa was called Nigel and he thought Nige was a funny nickname. Debatable. He tells me her eyes are now actually green. Apparently all kittens have blue eyes before they get their permanent eye colour at around six weeks. No way! Come to think of it – 'Greeny?!' doesn't sound as good. Sounds like another name for a bogey, in fact. Yuck! Who wants a bogey sitting in their lap?

Maybe Jake isn't so bad after all? If he really had no idea that I was in the pet shop that day, then I

may have misjudged him. Perhaps I should give him the benefit of the doubt.

'Hah! This is the culprit! This was my bottle!' I say, holding a plastic bottle up in the air.

Jake asks me how I could possibly know that and I show him the hole in the top of one side. As he remembers Mrs Chen having the lemonade-soaked J-cloth flung in her face he bursts out laughing. I start giggling too, and soon we are both belly-laughing, recounting everything in detail.

'Who knew placid Mrs Chen could get so angry? And she's supposed to be a soft touch!' says Jake.

'Can you imagine if it had been Mrs Mannan?!' I giggle. 'We would definitely have been expelled!'

'Her moustache would have been dripping from the edges!' Jake laughs. 'Catty and Pillar would have been foaming from their mouths!'

We are both in hysterics now. And then I wonder how he knows about Catty and Pillar.

Only me and Keziah know about that. That is our thing. He tells me that when I was off school he had been next to Keziah in the lunch queue and Mrs Mannan had walked past with a bit of food stuck to her upper lip. Jake had commented that her 'tache must have been hungry and Keziah had said, 'The Hungry Caterpillar!' He'd laughed and then she had told him about how we call the two bits of her moustache Catty and Pillar. Keziah

hasn't told me this. Not only are Catty and Pillar our thing, me and Keziah always call moustaches 'taches.

Just as I am about to erupt in a fit of rage I remember that jealousy is an ugly trait. Now is not the time to get angry at Jake for trying to muscle in on my best friend. We have only just declared a truce. Maybe it's better to keep him as a friend rather than an enemy. A frenemy.

CHAPTER 16

Frenemies

The next morning, the events of the day before feel like a surreal dream. Hating Jake, shaking Jake's hand, helping Jake stay on *Brainbusters*, not being sure about Jake. Then there were Selina's Mentos, the lemonade explosion, Mrs De Souza's office, Ms Krantz being proven innocent and the revelations about Bluey. *Everything today will seem mundane in comparison,* I think, as I munch on my Shreddies at breakfast.

Look! There's an elephant in the school playground!

Meh . . . That's nothing compared to yesterday

At school me and Jake are *kind of* getting along. He even thanks me for confessing and saving his place on *Brainbusters*. We aren't being overly friendly or anything like that (I am still a little wary of him), but we aren't ignoring each other or being mean or competitive over stuff any more. We don't sit together at lunch or hang out at break time, but we are polite, nice and helpful to each other. I lend him my sharpener when his pencil is blunt. He tells me an answer I don't know. I get him a handout when getting one for myself and so on . . .

I *even* laugh at a joke he makes about Catty and Pillar. We have reached a stalemate and it seems to work well.

At break time everyone wants to know what happened to us the previous afternoon. Even kids from the other Year Five class have heard the legend of the lemonade explosion. It's like we've gained some new cool, rebellious status. Suzie Ashby offers round a bag of pickled onion Monster Munch (which is uncharacteristically nice of her) and everyone sits on the lower rungs of the large climbing frame and the tarmac listening to us re-enact the tale. Team 'We Don't Want To Be Expelled' has reconvened to entertain the crowds.

Like a well-rehearsed stand-up comedy act, we play out the whole story between us, complete with sound effects and a few creative tweaks. In our *adapted* version of the story we are *almost* expelled by Mrs De Souza, who is intent on making us cry, but we both bravely hold out. Just as she is about to ring our parents to come and take us home I say, 'Punish me, not him,' pointing at Jake, who then says, 'No! Punish me, not her!' and, like the true heroes we are, we both try to take the blame and save the other. Mrs De Souza, realising we have courage and guts and loyalty (three important qualities in a person) and that the school would suffer without us, decides there will be no expulsion and no punishment.

Our growing audience is hooked on our every word. Some Year Six students even join in. Lots of people ask questions:

'What is her office like?'

'Did you soak the floor?'

'Did you apologise or did you stand your ground, as it was all an accident?'

. . . and so on. We finish our little masterclass in rebellion and even get a small round of applause. It feels good.

The rest of the week is fairly uneventful, but during Friday's double PE there is an unexpected turn of events. It has started raining outside, so the other Year Five class joins us inside for PE in the gym.

When it's wet we usually play team games and today is no exception. It's the only time I actually enjoy PE, since I'm not exactly sporty. Mr Edwards, the PE teacher, makes our class the red team and Kestrel class the green team, which I much prefer to boys against girls (bit sexist if you ask me, I mean, what is this – the Stone Age?!). Worse than that is that when two team leaders are picked they take it in turns to choose who'll be on their team.

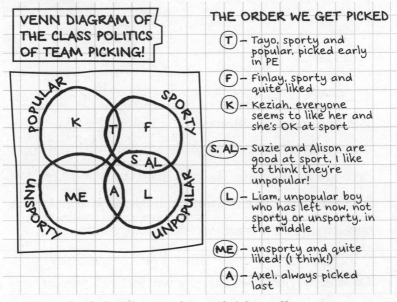

VENN DIAGRAM OF THE CLASS POLITICS OF TEAM PICKING!

POPULAR
SPORTY
UNSPORTY
UNPOPULAR

K
T
F
S AL
ME
A
L

THE ORDER WE GET PICKED

(T) – Tayo, sporty and popular, picked early in PE

(F) – Finlay, sporty and quite liked

(K) – Keziah, everyone seems to like her and she's OK at sport

(S, AL) – Suzie and Alison are good at sport, I like to think they're unpopular!

(L) – Liam, unpopular boy who has left now, not sporty or unsporty, in the middle

(ME) – unsporty and quite liked! (I think!)

(A) – Axel, always picked last

If you're left till near the end, it's really humiliating.

OK, Tayo, your turn to pick and then we'll start

Hope he picks me . . . there's no one left

I think I've got enough people already, sir

We all put on red and green bibs to show whether we are Sparrowhawks or Kestrels and then have to do a timed obstacle course around the gym against the other class.

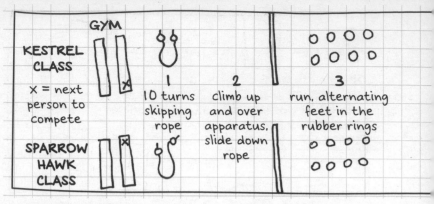

Excitement levels are at fever pitch. Everyone shouts and cheers on their classmates. Keziah is up first against Martha Masters from the other Year Five class. We take a comfortable lead when Martha trips up as she is trying to do ten turns of the skipping rope. I always think that skipping is dodgy since everyone tries to get away by doing fewer turns than they're supposed to and Mr Edwards can't competently watch both teams at once. He's meant to add on time for cheating – but he never really does.

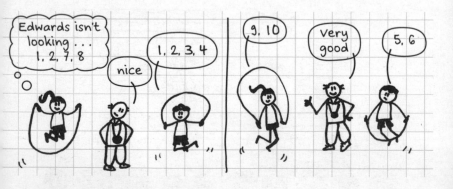

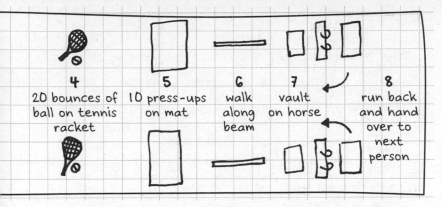

4	5	6	7	8
20 bounces of ball on tennis racket	10 press-ups on mat	walk along beam	vault on horse	run back and hand over to next person

By the time it is my go, we are behind – typical – but I get round the course in no time at all, even managing to get up and over the climbing apparatus without much difficulty. I slide down the rope and find I have somehow managed to lessen the gap with the other team. I'm actually not bad at climbing as I'm light and nimble. What makes me bad at sport is I'm not especially coordinated and, worse still, have zero stamina. I often appear really good at stuff for a very short while until I get tired five minutes later and give up!

Next up is Jake against a new boy from the other class. He manages to draw us even, so we are level pegging when Suzie Ashby goes up against Priti Prashad.

The tension is mounting as they both balance precariously on their respective beams.

'Come on, Suzie, you can do it!' I shout.

I know. That's not something you'll hear coming out of my mouth very often, but I really want our team to win. *Go, Sparrowhawks, go!*

Suzie and Priti jump down at exactly the same time to cheers of encouragement from the crowd – but Priti looks as though her ankle has given way. She quickly regains her balance, though, and the race is back on . . .

'Ace it, Ashby!' yells Tayo.

Suzie is loving this.

'Kestrel is Bestrel!' chants the other class.

Seriously? Bestrel? Is that the best they can come

up with? They
don't deserve to
win with slogans
like that.

The girls run,
still neck and neck,
gearing up to vault
over the horse.

Just as Priti jumps,
her bad ankle lets her down and she goes crashing
over. Trying to use her arm to break her fall, she
accidentally smacks it into the leg of the horse and
it makes an audible crunch. Everyone gasps. Priti
lies on the floor, clutching her arm and crying out
in pain. The mood of
the whole gym switches
from sheer excitement
and euphoria to utter
horror in a split second.

Mr Edwards tells us
all to sit down cross-legged on the gym floor and
chat quietly among ourselves. He tries to see if Priti
can move or not and whether it is perhaps just a
sprain. But Priti is in too much pain, so he tells us to

go to the cloakrooms, get changed and head to our next class after fifteen minutes.

Keziah (whose dad Paul is a nurse) says she thinks Priti has definitely twisted her ankle and possibly fractured her arm too. By the end of the day Priti hasn't returned to class and rumours are circulating that she has been taken to hospital in an ambulance. I don't want to jump to any conclusions, though, because rumours are often unreliable.

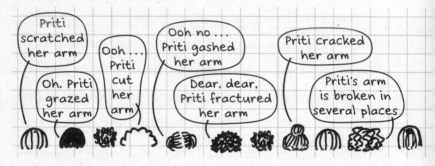

This is going to sound awful but I can't help but think that if Priti is injured, perhaps she won't be able to go on *Brainbusters* next week. Poor Priti . . . but she'll get over it. The school will give her some other prize instead. This could be my chance! My bird-poo luck! I feel terrible and do hope Priti is OK, but I also want to be on that quiz SO badly. They won't be able to have another science competition, so how will they pick? Would it be random?

If so, I have a one in fifty-eight chance.

$$P(BB) = \frac{\text{no. new contestants to be picked}}{\text{no. in year} - (\text{Priti} + \text{Jake})} = \frac{1}{60 - (1+1)}$$

$$= \frac{1}{60 - 2} = \frac{1}{58}$$

Not great odds. We have already had a general knowledge test this week and I got all the answers right. That has to qualify me, doesn't it?

I can't sleep that night and am up at 6 a.m. the next morning, raring to go to school.

When I get there, I dicover that, sure enough, Keziah is right (as always!). Mrs Mannan announces that Priti has sprained her ankle and broken her arm. Now that *is* an announcement. She will be on strong painkillers for a while and won't be able to go on *Brainbusters*. AMAZING. **Yeeesssss!!!** Oh, and poor Priti . . .

163

'I could be your partner on *Brainbusters* now,' I whisper to Jake, giving him a big wink and waving my test mark in his face. Having him on-side would be better all round. He tries to mouth something to me, but I can't understand what he is saying. He tries again, but Mrs Mannan beats him to it. 'This means, Jake, that your new partner on *Brainbusters* will be Leo Mason from Kestrel class, who was, of course, runner-up in the science competition.'

My heart sinks. Jake already knew. He had been told after registration. I try to style it out by putting on a fake smile, as I don't want him to see how upset I am. I'm pretty sure there is no hiding it, though. Arghhh! I forgot all about Leo's dumb Pringles-tube telescope or whatever it was. The bird poo has failed me after all.

Heartbreaking.

CHAPTER 17

Ponies Aren't Baby Horses

9.30 a.m. – Leo Mason isn't going to be on *Brainbusters*. Apparently his mum would rather he wasn't on TV, because of something to do with his dad, who she's no longer with. Anyway, the point is that there's a vacancy up for grabs. A new day, a new start! I ask Mrs Mannan how they'll choose who will go in his place and suggest to her that the general knowledge test results would be a good way to decide. She says it's something she's going to discuss with the other staff at break time and that I should get back to learning about the Norman Conquest instead of blathering on about modern-day quiz shows.

11 a.m. – turns out that another six people in the year got full marks in the test so my *Brainbusters* appearance is far from a done deal. So frustrating!

12 p.m. – Jake is called to Mr Hasting's office. I'm dying to know why. Is it to do with *Brainbusters*? What else could it possibly be about?

12.20 p.m. – Jake comes to lunch late. Some people are already on dessert. (It's actually really nice today: a vanilla bread and butter pudding with dark chocolate salted caramel sauce. A bit posh for school dinners but **VERY TASTY**.) I ask him what Mr Hastings wanted and he said he was given some forms from the TV company for his parents to fill out. I ask him who the other contestant will be. He just shrugs.

12.27 p.m. – on further interrogation Jake tells me

who the other six people were who

got top marks in the test . . .

1. Priti Prashad – well,

she's out of the running.

2. Richie Stott –

have only

encountered

him once in the

library. Seems

nice. Says the

letter 'W' when he means to say the letter 'R'.

3. Keiko Nguyen – my sister Roubi knew her

brother because they

were on the school

council together. Her

brother is **REALLY** clever.

4. Clement Boudin – he moved here from France

at the end of Year One and couldn't speak **ANY**

English. Since then he

has come on leaps and

bounds, as you can see.

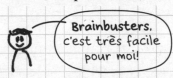

5. Jake – typical (he probably copied bits off me).

6. Me – I definitely copied bits off Jake!

When I say 'bits' it was actually only two bits and one I already knew the answer to.

Q1. What is the sixth planet from the sun?

A. Saturn.

Obviously I know this! I just made an entire nearly edible solar system! But in my rush I had written Jupiter. In fact, I have a very easy method to just speed up naming planets . . .

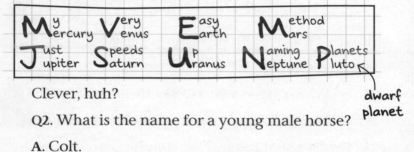

Clever, huh?

dwarf
planet

Q2. What is the name for a young male horse?

A. Colt.

I've heard of a colt and I know it was a horse, but I wasn't sure exactly what type. Since then I've looked up and learnt all the different types of horses . . .

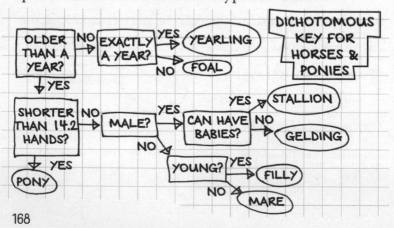

A pony is just a short horse! Who knew?! I know people often think they're baby horses, but no. A horse below 14.2 hands (147 cm) is a pony, NOT a horse. I know! Horses are measured in hands. How weird. What's wrong with centimetres or inches or feet? Oh yeah. Oops. Feet.

Ponies must be the only animals that have a whole new name just because they're short. Imagine being a horse all your adult life, then one day someone clips your hooves and you get a millimetre shorter and drop below the 14.2-hand threshold and suddenly you turn into a pony!! You're no longer a horse! So weird. Imagine if full-grown humans under 160 cm were all called mumans instead. Totally weird. My mum would be a muman.

1 p.m. – Mrs Mannan takes class as usual. The suspense is killing me. They'll need to pick someone soon. The show is in a few days' time! Today is Friday and it's being filmed on Tuesday!!!

2 p.m. – I can't concentrate on my work. Jake is acting a bit weird but I can't really pinpoint why.

2.45 p.m. – school ends in forty minutes and still NOTHING!

2.55 p.m. – I am called to Mr Hastings's office! Of the six people who scored full marks in the test, all the others are in Kestrel class apart from me and Jake. Have they been called from their class too? Am I about to take a sudden-death quiz challenge against them to determine who will go on *Brainbusters*?

2.56 p.m. – I knock on Mr Hastings's door and am told to enter. I'm hoping he is not having a strict day. I go inside and am the only one in there. Have the others been and gone? Is he seeing us one by one? Is he interviewing each person separately so he can make his decision?

He smiles at me. Phew. He's not having a strict day.

'Aaah, Cookie, sit down. You'll be aware that your fellow class member Jake Kay is going on *Brainbusters* to represent the school but needs a team partner. Since you got full marks in the recent class test, the teaching staff decided you and the other top scorers should all be in the running.' He pauses.

Yes? And? Is it me? Or is it Richie Stott? Then it'll be all boys. He might get his Ws and Rs confused. Not good for a letter-based quiz show.

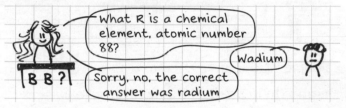

Do I have to jump through more hoops? Come on, put me out of my misery.

'We asked Jake to choose who he would like to partner up with . . .'

Great. So now I'm last on the waiting list, but if the others all break an arm, I'm through?

'. . . and he chose you. Congratulations!'

Typical! Just bring me here to dash my hopes, stamp on my drea— Wha—? You ARE kidding me?! Really?! Yeessss!!! I am about to burst. **HURRAH!!!!**

I can't believe it.

Only days ago I was in the head teacher's office on the verge of expulsion and now I am in the deputy head's office hearing **THIS!** Mr Hastings gives me a quick form to fill out about myself for the show's producers. **SO AMAZING**. The rollercoaster ride of trying to get on *Brainbusters* has finally come to an end. Unless I break my arm. Which I won't.

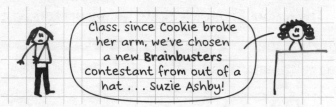

I decide I will have to be extra careful between now and then. I run all the way back to class as quickly (and as safely) as possible.

The school has already rung my parents to check they are happy for me to go on the show. They give me a letter to take home and get them to sign. I tuck it away in my bag (precious cargo!).

I can't believe it. I am going to be on TV.

I AM GOING TO BE ON TV!!!!!!!!!

WOO-HOO!!!!!!!!!

Everyone is getting their stuff from the cloakroom to leave. I run over to Jake and throw my arms round him, squeezing him tight. He looks weirded out.

'I love you!' I yelp, clinging on to him for what is probably longer than necessary. Dunno why I said that, cos I don't.

'Why didn't you tell me?' I cry out dramatically, (and ecstatically).

The school had to clear it with my parents first to avoid another duff announcement like the one they made about Leo Mason. Jake had been sworn to secrecy, even though he had known since lunchtime. This is epic. I run off to tell Keziah. Epic!!!!! Keziah screams with delight; she couldn't be more pleased for me. **EPIC!!!!!**

That weekend Jake and I decide to revise. We are in and out of each other's houses, on the internet, heads in encyclopaedias, testing each other, looking up capital

cities, studying the periodic table, memorising the map of the world. We are in **SERIOUS** training.

We are both enjoying our mission to absorb all the world's knowledge. Better still, we really get on. We like the same TV shows, have the same sense of humour . . . we are actually on the same wavelength. For instance . . .

1. We both like long words. In fact, he taught me a good one just now: ***defenestrate***. It means to throw out of a window.

2. We are both messy and find tidy people can often be boring and annoying.

TIDY PERSON . . .

COOKIE . . .

My books are all in alphabetical order

I know where everything is!!

3. We are both agnostic (not sure if God exists), even though our parents don't know!

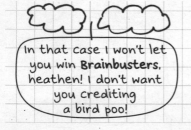

In that case I won't let you win **Brainbusters**, heathen! I don't want you crediting a bird poo!

At Jake's house his parents bring piles and piles of reference books up to his bedroom. His sister, Helen, offers to teach us all about horses, which we politely decline (as I already know my stallions from my geldings). His brother Will is a whizz on the piano, so teaches us to distinguish our minims from our crotchets (which I didn't already know). His youngest brother, Archie, just sits in the corner gurgling and dribbling. There isn't much he can teach us!

At my house my parents keep feeding us – everything from samosas and chicken drumsticks to nuts and chopped fruit. Brain food. My mum is always happiest when feeding people. She

can conjure up a feast out of nowhere and has no qualms about snacking in between meals! Roubi

even pops her head in and gives us a quick overview of the UK political system.

By the end of the weekend my head is so full of knowledge it is about to explode. *Brainbusters* won't know what's hit it!!!

CHAPTER 18

A Fishy End

7 a.m. on Monday, lying in bed, I feel invincible. I woke up at 6.53 a.m. and beat my alarm. WINNER! I wake up every morning now feeling all warm and happy when I remember . . . I am going to be on *Brainbusters*! Very few people in the world can say that. I can now switch on the TV again without fear of the show coming on. In fact, I *want* to see it. I no longer have to get angry at the thought of general knowledge quizzes and I *even* had a good swan dream last night. Life is **GREAT**.

It was the same dream I've had before where me and Keziah (who is also sometimes Jake – the way weird stuff happens in dreams) win *Brainbusters* and all the teachers love us and we win loads of stuff. This time, however, I look up as the quiz-show host congratulates us and notice the whole audience is made up of clapping swans, and they're all really pleased for me. None of them chase me. Life is **GREAT**.

Later that day in the school playground I tell Keziah about the word 'defenestrate', which she **LOVES**. When we sat next to each other Keziah and I used to have this thing about finding cool new words. We had a monthly list where we added all our favourites. The weirder, the better. It started in Year Three when we were laughing in class and the teacher, Mr Rai, told us to 'stop guffawing'. We had no idea what he was talking about, so he made us look it up in a dictionary.

guffaw *noun* /gəˈfɔː/
A loud and
hearty laugh.

We *guffawed* a lot back then. It often got us separated, especially in Year Four by Mrs Mannan. Terrible teaching method if you ask me – Keziah and I only ever have *intelligent* conversations that can only be *furthering* our education.

Some of my favourite words from our list are:

Troglodyte – someone who lives in caves.

Entomophagy
– when people
eat insects.

Arachibutyrophobia – the fear of peanut butter sticking to the roof of the mouth.

There are so many different phobias but this is my favourite. It's actually a thing. A proper condition that people have. Can you believe it? It's nuts! Get it?! Nuts!

Keziah tells me Axel used a good word the other day: *schadenfreude*. It's German and it means when you get satisfaction from someone else's bad luck. Axel's parents are German. He used it when Mrs Chen got the J-cloth flung in her face.

He doesn't like her very much because she always gives him really low marks, but that's because he's not very good at science!

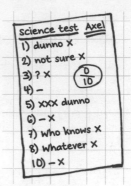

'His words, not mine,' says Keziah.

I laugh, then pause . . . and then do something really dumb.

I accuse Keziah of being better friends with Axel than me these days. I don't even know why I say it. I don't even believe it. Then *she* says, what about me and Jake? So then I say, *I* wasn't the one who told him about Catty and Pillar. So then *she* says I am being immature. So then *I* storm off. So then *she* looks pretty annoyed. So then *I* feel terrible. Keziah never gets annoyed at *anything*; she usually laughs stuff off. I know I am totally in the wrong. I have to make up with her. I no longer feel invincible.

In morning lessons, I am feeling low about the Keziah situation. Jake, on the other hand, is in a really good mood, making funny jokes,

being cheeky . . . generally on a pre-*Brainbusters* high. I try to join in but feel bad about being mean to Keziah.

At lunchtime I can't find Keziah anywhere. Selina tells me how excited she is about me going on *Brainbusters*. I ask her how she knows and she says she bumped into Keziah in Argos at the weekend. Keziah had excitedly told her everything. Selina tries to give me extra chips but I'm not hungry.

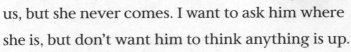

You can't solve everything with chips, Selina

I sit with Axel in the lunch hall in the hope Keziah will join us, but she never comes. I want to ask him where she is, but don't want him to think anything is up.

Usually Keziah and I know each other's every move, but I had stormed off before I could even say, 'See you at lunch?'

Worse still, I chat to Axel and he's really sweet, even though he looks at his plate the whole time we speak.

Axel is funny but I wish he'd stop looking at his plate. What's wrong with my face?

It's fish and chips for lunch and I tell him that

181

since I got my goldfish I feel weird about eating fish. He says that his mum grows carrots, but it doesn't put him off eating them – it is only the taste that does that! I laugh, even though I'm not totally sure if it is supposed to be funny or not. He asks if my fish are from *Woof, Miaow, Squea*k and tells me that when he was younger his nan took him there loads. She called it the free zoo!

Axel is a dark horse. (Or should I say pony? He is quite short, after all!!!) Although he seems quiet and awkward, he's actually **REALLY** funny. I **REALLY** like him. I should have known. Keziah is always a good judge of character. *Where is she?*

That evening Jake comes over to my house for our last revision session before the big day tomorrow. We sit in the garden testing each other, surrounded by textbooks and lists and maps but I can't concentrate on anything, probably because I

am worried about Keziah.
I am in a really foul mood.
I never fall out with
Keziah. Who would have
thought I could possibly
feel like this the day before
my *Brainbusters* TV debut?

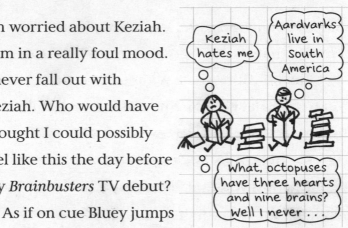

As if on cue Bluey jumps
over the fence and starts lapping up water from our
pond. Bluey – my saviour. It's like she knows I could
do with a cuddle right now. Yay, Bluey!

But as I bend over the pond to pick her up I
notice the pond is empty. *Totally empty.*

I start panicking and searching with my eyes
down into the murky depths of the brown water.
Where are my fish? Are they hidden at the bottom?
Behind some pond weeds? Who am I kidding? The
pond is too shallow for that.

I double-check . . . and triple-check . . . and
quadruple-check . . . and quintuple-check! And
check even more than that.

No Mercury, no Venus, no Mars, no Jupiter, no
Saturn, no Neptune, no Pluto. No fish.

No. This can't be! My fish have gone.

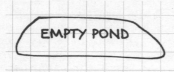
EMPTY POND

Vanished into thin air. No longer visible. Gone. Where are they?

My stomach tightens and I feel like I am going to be sick. Bluey looks up at me with her now green eyes – *then licks her lips and swallows.* Was that a fish tail sticking out of your mouth just then, or did I imagine it? Am I going mad?

It's likely you're mad . . . cardigan feeding, bathing your ball, imagining I can talk!

How could you? I think, sickened to the core. I am over Bluey. Jake can have his stupid Nigel. I let go of the horrible cat and storm over to Jake, who is memorising a list of famous Baltic landmarks.

'HOW COULD YOU LET YOUR STUPID GREEN-EYED CAT EAT ALL MY FISH? DON'T YOU FEED HER PROPERLY? DON'T YOU KEEP AN EYE ON HER?' I yell through tears, unable to contain my anger.

SOLITARY CONFINEMENT

* HIGH SECURITY *
* HIGH-RISK PRISONER *
* BEWARE!! *

'SHE IS A MASS MURDERER AND NEEDS LOCKING UP!'

Jake opens his mouth to speak but I don't want to hear it. I don't want to hear *anything*. I pick up my stuff and run into the house, screaming, 'You're the most annoying boy in the world! Leave now! You're trespassing!!'

The Cold Shoulder War is back on.

There is only one person whose voice I *do* want to hear and who *can* make me feel better right now and she probably hates me. I ring Keziah and tell her I am sorry about Axel who *is* really nice, and that I was worried

Keziah hates me. My fish are gone . . . I have NOTHING!

when she wasn't at lunch and that I really want to apologise and please would she forgive me?

There is a pause . . .

Then Keziah laughs her warm, infectious laugh and I know everything is OK. She had been at a dentist's appointment and doesn't hate me at all. She teases me, and says she is flattered I was jealous of Axel! I laugh and cry at the same time and tell her all about my fish. I sob and sob and sob.

First I had no pets. Then I had seven. I loved them. Now they're gone. And now I have no pets again.

I feel so empty and miserable. Keziah listens and says everything I need to hear to make me feel a little bit better. I thank her and she tells me I have to put it out of my mind for now and get a good night's sleep, so I can focus on my big day tomorrow and do what I'm best at . . . being amazing! I hang up the phone in a much better place than I had been when I had first rang her.

Man, I love that girl.

CHAPTER 19

Brainbusters

The next day, we don't even have to go into school. We are picked up from home by the TV company and taken straight to the studios, with Mr Hastings accompanying us. My excitement is bittersweet. I am still in mourning after my horrific loss and can't help but feel miserable. The weird thing is, my misery is tinged with the odd pang of excitement and nerves when I think about actually being on telly in real people's living rooms!!

We have been told to wear brightly coloured clothes with no heavy patterns or brand logos and to bring two spare tops in case of emergency (like a drink spillage or a tear or a random swan attack, perhaps).

Bah!! . . . They must have made up the no-logo rule after that boy's 'winner' T-shirt. Guess that rules this top out!!

LOSER

Jake and I had decided we would coordinate by wearing matching outfits, but I guess that is out of the window now. We are also supposed to bring a team mascot. I was going to bring Keziah's fluffy-ball monster, which she has clipped to her

Keziah's fluffy-ball monster

I'm better than bird poo

school bag, but I didn't get a chance to grab it after we fell out yesterday. I will have to find something else instead.

Mum makes me a massive breakfast. Brain food. She has also made me what is practically a packed lunch, only she calls it a 'light snacks bag'.

I'm starving!

Light snacks?!! Who does she think I am? King Kong?!!

CONTENTS OF LIGHT SNACKS BAG

apples (probably one for Jake and me . . .) same with eggs ×2

boiled eggs (weird, I know!) ×2

Pringles — original flavour (I prefer salt & vinegar)

zip-lock bag of samosas too spicy for pre-TV debut

bananas — these will inevitably go black and mushy in the bag — yuck!!

satsumas / clementines / tangerines — not sure of the difference. Not sure why 3! ×3

Twiglets

pack of mini Babybels

2x bags of cashews

KitKat — 4 sticks (didn't even make it to the car!!)

Tupperware of egg-fried rice!!?!?

coronation chicken sandwiches (no explanation needed)

small box of raisins

Everyone is being very careful around me. Roubi is being really nice to me and Dad offers to get me some new fish! New fish?? What does he think they are? Inanimate objects? You can't just replace them! They had personalities . If we all died, would he just shrug and adopt three new kids and act like nothing had happened?!!

Don't worry, dear — we can get three new girls, or even a boy or two!

ADOPTION AGENCY

OPEN

It's quite exciting

I guess he's right and there'll probably be more choice!

Roubi says it's tough having pets. They inevitably die before you and so you're just setting yourself up for sadness. 'Unless you get a tortoise', she adds. 'They can live up to 150 years!'

Mum says it's tougher having children. Your life revolves around them: you have to wipe up their snot, poo and vomit, and then they grow up, don't want you around and just ask for money the whole time!

She says my eldest sister, Nahid, had briefly come back from university yesterday lunchtime as she had an internship interview in central London. She'd dumped all her washing, wiped out Mum's purse, then left and wouldn't even take some light snacks with her!

Light snacks? I think, looking down at my plastic bag containing a small banquet for two.

The light snacks do actually come in handy as the journey takes **AGES**. We are all driven in a people carrier. Jake and I sit silently in the back while Mr Hastings sits up front next to the driver. Although Jake and I aren't talking to each other, it doesn't look too obvious since we both have our heads in books, so it appears as if we are just revising. Jake is reading *1,000 Animal Facts*, while I pretend to look at a mini atlas. Mr Hastings is reading too: a book on assertiveness called *How to Stand Up for Yourself and Still Win the Respect of Others*. Maybe not an ideal read in front of your students!

To maintain the silence I try to eat my snacks quietly,

which isn't easy when you're munching on Pringles, the noisiest crisps ever invented. I keep having to quietly dissolve them in my mouth.

I feel a bit bad about not talking to Jake, but then again his cat *did* kill my fish. Last night Keziah said she thought it could have been a fox, but I'm pretty sure foxes don't eat pond fish; they head straight for the rubbish bags and feast on remnants of chicken drumsticks and spare ribs.

The foxes round our way are so brazen and confident. I once saw one stopping traffic to cross the road in broad daylight as if it were a human being. It even used the zebra crossing!

My poor fish. I hope it was a quick and painless end. I had been so busy revising over the weekend that I didn't even give them the love and attention they deserved in our final moments together. I used to find it so relaxing and calming watching them innocently swimming about.

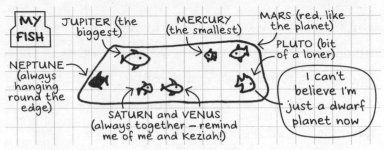

MY FISH

JUPITER (the biggest)

MERCURY (the smallest)

MARS (red, like the planet)

PLUTO (bit of a loner)

NEPTUNE (always hanging round the edge)

SATURN and VENUS (always together – remind me of me and Keziah!)

I can't believe I'm just a dwarf planet now

Rest in peace, my little fishies. So sorry about Nigel. If it was Nigel. It has to be Nigel! For one thing, Jake's house is on the same side as our pond, and what's more I've seen Nigel dining from it as though it is an eat-as-much-as-you-like buffet. Well, drinking from it. It has to be Nigel. I think.

After what feels like hours, we arrive at the TV studios and finally the whole *Brainbusters* dream begins to feel real. We are met by the producer, Mel, who is in charge of everything, and a 'chaperone' called Nicky. Nicky has to stay with us at all times and make sure we are OK. It is a bit like being famous and having a personal assistant.

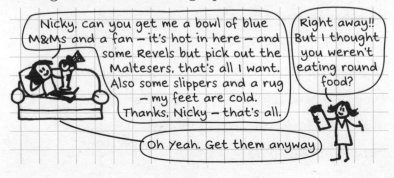

Nicky, can you get me a bowl of blue M&Ms and a fan – it's hot in here – and some Revels but pick out the Maltesers, that's all I want. Also some slippers and a rug – my feet are cold. Thanks, Nicky – that's all.

Oh yeah. Get them anyway

Right away!! But I thought you weren't eating round food?

She keeps asking us if we want bottles of water or snacks. She even has to come with us if we need the loo. Not actually inside – she just has to wait by the door. Maybe in case we fall into the toilet and can't get out?

We are also taken on a little tour of the studios. The corridors are all lined with cheesy photos of cheesy people off the telly. The *Brainbusters* studio itself looks so much smaller in real life than on TV, although the ceiling is really high with loads of lights hanging off it. Very high-tech. Get it? High?

We also go into the 'gallery', a room with loads of TV screens each showing different camera angles to the director. After that we meet the presenter, Maddy Mitchell, who is just as nice in real life as she is on the TV. She even says she likes my top!

I think the producer notices our silence because she comments that we must be saving up all our energy for the show. She then points out the team we are up against, who look really annoying – and like they are having the time of their lives.

After the 'tour' we are taken to our dressing room, which

has our names on the door!!!

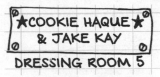

Inside there is a wardrobe, sofa, TV and a dressing table with lights round the mirror just like you'd expect. We even have our own little shower room with a toilet. If you slept on the sofa, you could practically live here! On the dressing table there is a bowl full of Celebrations and Heroes. Jake and I make a beeline for it and shove a couple in our mouths.

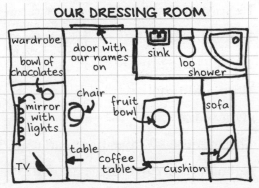

I want to laugh but have to contain myself as I am still angry about my fish.

A lady from the wardrobe department comes to look at our clothes. She says that we both look great and can stay in what we are already wearing but that she will need to iron my top and pin our name badges on. She must notice that I look offended because she explains that they always have to iron tops, even if they don't seem creased.

So why iron it then?

Then a researcher comes in and asks us questions about ourselves. We both have to act enthusiastic and as though we like each other. Easier said than done.

WHAT WE SAID . . .

We met at nursery and have been best friends since

Yeah, we are inseparable, two peas in a pod

WHAT WE MEANT . . .

We've known each other a couple of weeks and hate each other!

Yeah, we're not on speaking terms, chalk and cheese

Soon it is lunchtime and Daisy Flowers the floor assistant (whose name I already knew!) pops her head round the door to tell us we can go to the canteen. She looks nothing

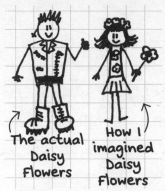

The actual Daisy Flowers

How I imagined Daisy Flowers

like I imagined she would. Hardly what you'd expect for someone called Daisy Flowers. She is covered in tattoos and piercings – nothing flowery about her!

I really want to ask her if she has sisters called Lily and Rose, but think it might sound stupid so don't bother. At lunch Jake takes the opportunity to try to speak to me but I really don't want to hear it. The last thing I want is a scene in the canteen – there might be famous people in here. I'm pretty sure I saw a weather presenter

weather presenter

fellow weather presenter

at the salad bar getting a bowl of cherry tomatoes.

The *Brainbusters* shows are shot back to back, four episodes a day. After lunch we are supposed to shoot our episode, but the show before ours is running late, which means Jake and I have to endure another hour sitting in the dressing room together in total silence. Mr Hastings has

decided to go and sit in the
studio audience, leaving poor
Nicky, our chaperone, sitting
awkwardly between us, trying
to make polite conversation.

I know my attitude isn't going to help us win
anything, but the nerves have seriously got to me. It
is all so real now, having seen the studio and Maddy
and our opponents. Just as I decide I should maybe
clear the air, Daisy pops her head round the door
again.

'The studio is ready for you now. It's showtime!'

CHAPTER 20

Blink and You'll Miss It

As we are leaving the dressing room Daisy asks if we have brought our mascots with us. The mascot! Arghhh! I **ALWAYS** forget something! Why would today be any different?

I look round the dressing room. There must be something I can use.

Jake has brought his: a fuzzy, grinning, tubby gorilla wearing a yellow T-shirt with 'You Can Do It!' written on it.

How nauseating.

'We can share mine,' he says. 'We're a team.'

Even more nauseating!

I don't have much choice in the matter.

'Er, we're sharing a mascot,' I say to Daisy through gritted teeth.

We sit in our places and test our buzzers as the wardrobe lady (who has unnecessarily ironed my top) pins red team badges on us with our names printed on in big lettering.

RED TEAM
Cookie Haque

I can feel the nerves kicking in. The lights are bright, but I can just about make out a small studio audience of around fifteen to twenty people. Mr Hastings is at the front, right in my eyeline. A make-up lady comes over and powders both our faces, and moves Jake's stupid sweeping side fringe out of his eyes with a comb, fixing it in place with a touch of hairspray.

'You both look lovely,' she says. 'Good luck!' I feel mildly sick.

I see Maddy about to sit in her seat. I must remember to get her autograph for Keziah. She stops as she walks past the other team and says to the girl: 'I really like your top.'

WHAT?!!!!! Like your top indeed! It's obviously just a thing she says to *everyone* as opposed to her actually liking my top.

Maddy Mitchell! You vacuous TV presenter.

'Thanks so much, Maddy. I wore my favourite one just for you,' the girl gushes.

Maddy sits down and the make-up lady starts spraying her hair, painting her lips and dabbing on blusher as she reads through her cue cards. *Waaaaah! This is all so real!* Daisy brings us each a glass of water we can sip on throughout the show. I feel really tense and down the lot in one go. I hope I won't need to pee in the middle of the quiz show.

'Stand by on studio floor,' calls out a voice, 'and roll opening titles!'

There it is: the catchy but annoying *Brainbusters* music. And so the show begins.

'Hello and welcome to *Brainbusters*! The show that puts you through your paces. So let's meet those clever faces! First up, the red team!'

Maddy turns to Jake first and asks him if he has any pets. He mentions he has a little kitten who

is only a few months old.

The audience all go *ahhhh*.

'Yes, she's very mischievous and a bit naughty! She loves clowning around.'

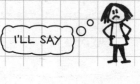

Maddy then asks him if he's brought a mascot and Jake says, 'Yes, this is Nigel. He's named after my grandpa.'

NIGEL?! AGAIN?! DO YOU CALL EVERYTHING NIGEL?!

'What a fab mascot! Which brings me on nicely to your teammate, Cookie . . .' says Maddy, smiling.

'Er, I don't have a mascot,' I blurt out, before Maddy has even asked anything, 'because, you see, well, it's a bird poo.'

Maddy looks confused and the audience laugh.

'You see, I got pooed on and my dad said bird poo means good luck, but I didn't want to scrape it up and keep it because that would be too weird. So I don't have a mascot, but hopefully the poo will bring me good luck.' The audience laugh some more.

Jake chips in. 'We're sharing Nigel; he's our team mascot. We're a team.'

yeah, you know all about team camaraderie . . . YOU FISH MURDERER!!

'OK,' says Maddy, 'that's great! Sharing is caring!

And Cookie, you've got some goldfish named after the planets, haven't you?'

No, they're dead, Jake's cat ate them all

'Yes, most of them have similar colouring to the planets they're named after, although Neptune is most definitely orange and not at all blue.'

Even though it isn't really funny the audience laugh. It feels nice they think I am funny. I like it. Sorry to like something at your expense, dead fish. I had totally forgotten that I filled out the 'about myself' section on the show's entry form on Friday afternoon *before* Nigel killed my fish. I can tell Jake feels bad about all this pet chat, and without even thinking I spontaneously give his hand a little squeeze behind the table and he gives mine a little squeeze back.

After Maddy introduces the yellow team, the quiz begins. It all happens so fast from then on. After such a long lead-up, it almost feels like a case of 'blink and you'll miss it'.

'OK, hands on your buzzers, teams. First question, what "F" is a baby horse?'

I know this! The answer is foal! But before I can even *think* about buzzing in, the other team gets in there first with the correct answer. I am going to have to up my game for the second question.

'What "E" is an alloy of silver and gold?'

What?! I have no idea. The other team buzz in again – but they think the answer is 'element' so the question passes over to us.

'Electrum,' says Jake – and he's right!

How on earth does he know that? I've never heard of *electrum* before. The next few questions go by in a blur. Soon round one is over and I haven't managed to score one single point. Frustratingly, I knew lots of the answers but I just wasn't fast enough. Jake on the other hand seems to have new a found confidence. He is on fire.

Maybe round two will be my time to shine . . .
unless my buzzer is broken, that is! Before I know
what I am doing I press it, even though the round is
over. Oops. The audience laughs.

'Cookie's keen for the next round!' says Maddy.

'Er, just checking my buzzer is working,' I say to
more audience laughter.

'No need to worry –
there's plenty of time
left, so you've still got
the chance to answer a
question.' Maddy smiles. I feel myself blushing.

Gee! Thanks for that,
Maddy . . . yes, in case
any members of the
studio audience or the
1000s of people at home
hadn't noticed yet . . .
I haven't answered ANY
questions right

'Now, Cookie, one of your hobbies is
making lists of long words, isn't it?'

Ugh! It sounds so square when read out like that,
but I couldn't think of anything else to put in the
hobbies section of the form.

county tennis
champ

potholing

scuba diving

OTHER TEAM'S HOBBIES   JAKE'S HOBBY

I don't really have any proper hobbies since I
stopped collecting stuff. I must be the world's most

BORING person. Well, after Suzie Ashby and Alison Denbigh.

doofus

Hang on . . . Don't Suzie and Alison do loads of after-school clubs?

horse riding

gymnastics

ballet

clarinet

abseiling

skiing

Doh!!

'Yes, the longer and weirder the better,' I reply, turning bright red with embarrassment. Luckily the audience laugh. They think I'm funny. I like them.

'Can you give us a good example?'

'Errr . . . defenestrate?'

'Great word, Cookie! What does it mean?'

'Well, if I say I want to defenestrate Jake, it would mean I want to throw him out of the window,' I reply.

More laughter from the audience.

Duh . . . I was lying, you fish killer!

Waah!! I thought you didn't want to throw me out the window

207

'I don't, though.'

Even more laughter from the audience.

If only I was as good at the actual quiz questions as I am at these ones!!

'Well, I hope you don't *defenestrate* me if the reds don't win today,' says Maddy. The audience laughs, again.

Stop stealing my jokes, Maddy!

The rest of the quiz is just as horrific for me as the first round. The yellow team win round two, drawing us even. While this makes me panic, it seems to spur Jake on to win rounds three and four. Unreal. We have won a load of books for the school library AND Jake has singlehandedly managed to get us to the final. Thank you, thank you, thank you, Jake! But I still want to throw you out of the window . . .

After Maddy has said goodbye to the yellow team, we have to choose which of us will play in the final round for the school's computer package. This isn't a buzz-in round. The team has to pick one person to play. Either me or Jake. And it will be against the clock. Maybe I have a chance here? Jake turns to me. '*You* can do it if you want,' he says. I'm not sure. I look at gorilla Nigel.

Could I?

Before I can decide whether it is a wise move or not, Maddy says, 'Looks like it's going to be Cookie! Give her a warm round of applause as she makes her way to the final game-board.'

The studio lights dim – all except for one spotlight centred on me. EEK!!! After the clapping dies down, I can practically hear the audience breathing. Talk about tension! What happens if I can't speak? What happens if I scream or wet myself or start crying? The aim is to make my way from one side of a grid of letters to the other, answering questions correctly.

'So, Cookie Haque, you know the rules! You have

one minute on the clock, and three lives, starting
from now! Let's brainbust!'

I can hear the clock ticking away. *Gulp.* I look at
the board and choose a letter . . .

'I'll have a "P", please, Maddy . . .'

Some audience
chuckles and titters. I
could actually quite easily
do a pee right now – bet they
wouldn't be laughing then!

Sahara, Gobi,
Kalahari
. . . doh!

What's that
running
down your
leg, Cookie?

You did say
I could have
a pee!

'Which "P" is the colourless
liquid containing the blood cells in
blood?' Maddy asks.

Well, it can't be plasma, I think, because that's
yellow. What else could it be, though? I rack my
brains for another 'P' as the seconds tick away on
the clock.

'Pass,' I say hurriedly, so as not to waste precious
time.

'The correct answer was plasma!' says Maddy.

WHAT??!! But plasma is *yellow*! I demand a
steward's inquiry! Is there some sort of conspiracy
against me? First you ask me about my dead fish
and then this! Agh! What am I doing thinking about

all this now? I'm in the middle of a quiz show! I can see there are only 46 seconds left on the clock. I need to pick another letter and fast.

'Can I have a "B", please, Maddy,' I say.

'What "B" is to cast a spell?' asks Maddy.

'Bind,' I say confidently. That is definitely the right answer. I'm sure I've seen the word used in a computer game Roubi was playing once. I have this one in the bag.

'Sorry,' says Maddy. 'The correct answer is "bewitch".'

Bewitch?! What?! What about wizards and druids? There's no such word as 'bewizard' or 'bedruid'. This answer would imply witches are the only things that can cast spells. I demand another steward's inquiry! What is wrong with this stupid quiz? But at least I have one life remaining and there are still 29 seconds left on the clock. I quickly pick my next letter.

"Can I have an "S", please, Maddy?'

'Which "S" is a bird that someone suffering from cygnophobia is scared of?' asks Maddy.

Cygnophobia? Wow! A phobia! I know about phobias. This is a sign! Hmm. What birds could people be scared of? Birds of prey. Wait! A sparrowhawk is a bird of prey! And it's the name of my class! Another sign! Amazing! It has to be sparrowhawk!

'Sparrowhawk!' I say confidently. At last I have got a question right!

'I'm afraid the answer is swan,' says Maddy, 'which means you've lost all three of your lives and that is the end of the game.'

Swans?!!! **I HATE SWANS!!!!**
I should have known. That is it.
The end of the show. And I haven't got a single question right.

'You didn't get the computing equipment,' says Maddy 'but you did win a bundle of books for the school AND you each get your own *Brainbusters* pen and backpack. Give them a huge round of applause – our winners this week, the red team!'

I still want to query Maddy's dodgy questions. Did she say clear liquid or colourless liquid? Because blood plasma is *yellow* and clear and NOT colourless. And bind *can* mean to cast a spell. I am still mulling it over as they whisk us off to get our signed photos of Maddy. Despite my frustration I remember to get one for Keziah too. We are then taken to the dressing room as they bring in the two teams for the next show.

'That was awful!' I say.

'You were great!' says Jake. 'The audience loved you! And we won! We beat the yellow team! Best of both worlds! Funny and winners!'

'Do you think?' I say.

'Definitely,' he replies.

CHAPTER 21

Bluey Again

'**Well** done, gang, you did it!' cries Mr Hastings, bursting into our dressing room. He doesn't seem to have registered my abysmal performance at all.

'You had me worried when the other team were so quick on the buzzer at the start, but you were just hustling, right?' He laughs. 'This will be great for the school newsletter!' He takes a picture of us holding up our *Brainbusters* backpacks and pens outside our dressing-room door.

'Say cheese!' he says as we grin inanely like we are in a mail-order catalogue.

MAIL-ORDER FORM (tick boxes as necessary)

Boy's crew-neck top	£12.99 ☐
Boy's denim fashion trousers	£20.99 ☐
Back-to-school **Brainbusters** backpack + pen	£15.99 ☐
Girl's rubbish hand-me-downs	FREE ☐

It feels sad leaving the TV studio after our little adventure away from school. Although I didn't answer any questions, no one seems to have noticed and it feels great being on the winning team. Everyone is so pleased for us. For the first time since my fish died, I feel really happy.

On the way out we walk past Daisy who gives us a big thumbs up. 'Well done, champs!' she says, high-fiving us.

I have to ask her. It's now or never . . .

'Hey, Daisy,' I say, 'do you have any sisters called Lily or Rose?'

'I've got two brothers, Mark and Dave,' she replies.

'Oh,' I say, a bit disappointed. 'I had always wondered . . .'

Wish I could knit me a leather jacket

But then she grins and adds that her grandma was called Primrose . . .

And that she wants to call her daughter Jasmine, if she ever has one.

Jasmine ~~Smith~~ Flowers

'But she won't have your surname,' I say.

'Oh yes she will. I'll make sure she does!' Daisy says, winking. Jasmine Flowers: I knew your name before you were born!

Everyone has been so kind to us that I pretty much feel like I *have* been successful on the show, which is good because in my mind I have been! *Plasma is definitely yellow and 'bind' is another word for casting a spell AND wizards can cast spells too. Not to mention druids, sorcerers and warlocks.*

In the car driving home Mr Hastings falls asleep and starts dribbling and snoring, which is a good source of amusement for a while.

I will be a stronger person

HOW TO BE STRONG

'How on earth did you know what electrum was?' I ask Jake.

'My mum had a ring made out of it, which she lost,' he explains. 'We found it a couple of months later in a lump of Play-Doh.'

'By the way,' I say, 'thanks for letting me share your gorilla mascot.'

'It's the least I could do,' he replies. 'I'm sorry Maddy asked you about your fish. Thanks for not letting on that they got killed by Nigel.'

I smile. 'I guess we're even now.'

'No more cold shoulder?' asks Jake hopefully.

'Definitely not,' I reply.

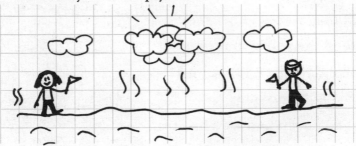

That evening Mum makes me my current favourite dinner – chicken biryani. It's a mildly spicy rice dish with bits of chicken and potato in. It's **SO YUM**.

(that's chicken biryani in case you didn't recognise it . . .)

Everyone is delighted we won *Brainbusters*. Dad says the bird poo obviously brought me good luck in the end.

'It didn't stop next door's cat eating my fish, though, did it?' I say.

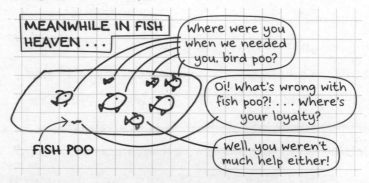

Mum then pipes up to say she spoke to Nahid on the phone, who told her she'd seen a heron by our pond that day. She had assumed it was eating slugs, since she didn't even know we had fish.

Plus she wasn't really paying much attention as she was late for her interview and was waiting for Mum to iron her top.

'What?!' I say as it all sinks in. A heron ate my fish?! Urgh! Typical. Annoying birds! Again! I hate herons!!! I HATE ALL BIRDS!! Swans, pigeons, herons, sparrowhawks – they're all the same.

URGH!! . . . Feathery freaks!!

কষাটে

('disgusting' in Bengali)

Roubi and I go on Google after dinner and find out that domesticated cats are highly unlikely to eat pond fish. In fact, most don't even like going in water – whereas herons are the number-one pond fish-eating culprit. It now seems so obvious. Bluey is innocent!

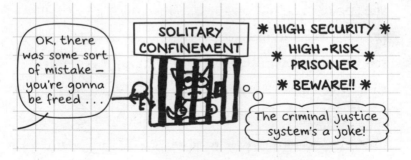

OK, there was some sort of mistake – you're gonna be freed . . .

SOLITARY CONFINEMENT

✳ HIGH SECURITY ✳
✳ HIGH-RISK PRISONER ✳
✳ BEWARE!! ✳

The criminal justice system's a joke!

At school the next day Jake and I wear our matching *Brainbusters* backpacks. Keziah and Axel come over and admire them. They want to know if we won and word that we did seems to get around incredibly fast.

Soon a small crowd has gathered round to ask us questions, just like when we'd been green-seated.

I give Keziah her signed Maddy photo. It reads: 'Keziah, I like your top, love Maddy xxx'.

It doesn't really. She actually wrote: 'Keziah, don't move to Solihull, love Maddy! xxx' but only cos I told her to write that after I noticed she had just put 'Best wishes, Maddy x' on everyone else's. I thought Keziah deserved more than that.

Keziah throws her arms around me. 'Thank you, Cookie! You rock! And guess what? I'm not supposed to tell anyone yet, but we're not moving to Solihull after all. Dad's being promoted in his current job so he doesn't need to take a new one!'

UNBELIEVABLE! KEZIAH MIGHT BE STAYING!

'You can't get rid of me that easily!' says Keziah.

'Phew!' I reply. 'Cos life would really suck without you!'

At lunchtime, when I see Selina, she already knows about our quiz-show victory. She has managed to get her hands on a freshly printed copy of the school newsletter with me and Jake grinning cheesily plastered on the front.

And thank goodness there is no mention that I didn't get one single question right. It could be much worse.

'Will you autograph it for me?' Selina teases. I laugh.

'No, I'm serious,' she says. 'I already got Jake to do it. I'm going to put it up in my house. I've cleared a space on the living-room wall.'

Selina + Bob

1935

Lovely . . . this old wedding pic can come down — just the right size space left to make room for the school newsletter. Smashing!!

'OK,' I say, bemused, and sign it as she piles a heap of extra chips on my plate.

SCHOOL NEWS *FREE COPY!!*
BRAINBUSTING
VICTORY!!!
Year Five students
Cookie Haque and
Jake Ray s...

Best wishes Selina —
Cookie x

For the first time ever Jake and I walk home from school together.

I take the opportunity to break the good news to him that Bluey isn't a fish killer after all. Everything

has been so hectic post-
Brainbusters that I'd clean
forgotten to tell him. I say I feel
terrible that I gave him such a
hard time without actually knowing the facts.

'I really didn't deserve to go on *Brainbusters*,' I
say. 'If I had been nicer and not given you the cold
shoulder, then maybe we would even have won the
computer. You wouldn't have felt that you had to
let me do the final game. We would probably have
walked it.'

'You did amazingly well considering you had
just been questioned about your murdered fish in
front of a live studio audience only a day after it had
happened,' Jake replies. 'And blood plasma *is* yellow!'

'And you can bind a spell,' I add.

'Hmm,' replies Jake. 'I'm not so sure about that one.'

'Anyway,' I say swiftly. 'Thanks for choosing me
to go on *Brainbusters* with you, Jake. I owe you.'

'No, you don't,' he says, laughing. 'To be honest,
you were the only kid that scored full marks in
their test who I actually knew! I'd only been at the
school for a few weeks – I'd never even heard of the
others!'

So your teammate options are Richie Stott, Kestrel class

Never heard of him

Keiko Nguyen, Kestrel class

Never heard of her

Clement Boudin, Kestrel

Never heard of him

Cookie Haque, Sparrowhawk

Oh!!!

'Thanks a bunch!!' I say, giggling. 'So that's the only reason you chose me. Charming!'

Jake goes quiet for a moment and looks at the floor.

'Look, Cookie, there's something I've got to tell you. Something I've been meaning to tell you for a while now.' He pauses. 'I just didn't know how . . .'

Ewww, please do NOT declare your undying love for me, Jake. Ugh . . . I do NOT feel the same. Gross. This would be SO messy . . .

Don't ask me to be bridesmaid

Oh . . . WAAAH! AWKWARD

'It's just that I *did* see your project plans on the kitchen counter when my parents came to dinner that Saturday night,' he says, his voice almost shaking. 'I had already tried out a couple of my own ideas and they had all failed. I was really stumped. When I saw your plans I realised I had all the materials to make a rotating planetarium and I just couldn't think of anything else. As I was new to the

224

school I badly wanted to make a good impression. I'm so sorry, Cookie, but you were right. I am a project thief.'

His lip is quivering and he seems like he is about to cry, a look I've never seen on Jake and never thought I would. I am totally speechless.

> I never thought I'd be lost for words. I mean, I always seem to have so much to say and there are never enough hours in the day and I'm always left wanting to say much more but I just can't fit it all in, but now I'm SPEECHLESS!

But I know exactly how Jake feels. He feels the same as I did in Mrs De Souza's office after the lemonade and Mentos confession.

And instead of feeling angry I am weirdly . . . *relieved*. I don't want him to be upset. I just want to put everything behind us and move on.

So I grin at him and say: 'Well, thank goodness you did. I knew my project idea was a winner!! If you hadn't stolen it, who knows what might have happened!?
It could have been lord knows who on *Brainbusters . . .*'

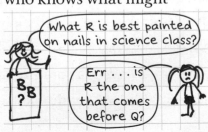

> What R is best painted on nails in science class?

> BB?

> Err . . . is R the one that comes before Q?

Jake laughs. 'My grandpa Nigel used to say, "Everything always works out the way it's meant to." Whatever that means.'

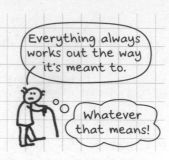

'Speaking of which,' he adds, 'it seems weird to call a female cat after a male grandpa. I reckon we should call her Bluey after all.'

'Even though her eyes are green?' I ask.

'My last head teacher was called Mr White but he was black, and my dentist's name is Mr Gardener. Oh yeah, and my cousin's called Grace and she is NOT graceful – so I think it's OK for Bluey to have green eyes.

'As you know, I already have a gorilla called Nigel that my grandpa gave me and he is a *he*. Plus, I really like the name Bluey.'

'You don't need to change her name,' I reply. 'You can call her whatever you want. She's not my cat.'

'Actually I've been thinking,' says Jake. 'I think we should *share* her. She really loves hanging out with both of us. Cats are independent and like to roam, so it makes sense for her to have two homes.'

I am speechless. Yet again.

> I never thought I'd be lost for words. I mean, I always seem to have so much to say and there are never enough hours in the day and I'm always left wanting to say much more but I just can't fit it all in, but now I'm SPEECHLESS!

This is the **MOST** amazing idea **EVER**. At last I will have my very own cat (shared with Jake, of course), and even better, a co-owner that I get on with! No more cuddling my mohair cardigan. No more being called mad by my sisters. I will be a **REAL** cat owner with a **REAL** cat. Life is good again. **REALLY GOOD**.

I am about to give Jake a huge hug when something warm trickles down my face. Is it a tear? Has it started to rain? I look down. A fresh bird poo has landed right in the middle of my cheek.

Jake laughs as part of it slides down my chin. 'That's supposed to give you good luck!' he says.

'Hmmmm. I'm not so sure!' I reply, then pause and think about it. 'Although actually . . . it looks like Keziah *is* staying after all, I was on the winning team on *Brainbusters* **AND** now I have a cat – my very own cat. Plus, I have a new next-door neighbour who is no longer the most annoying boy in the world. In fact, if he plays his cards right, he could be a very good friend. So yeah, maybe it does. Thank you, bird poo.'

APPENDIX*

HOW TO MAKE A LEMONADE FOUNTAIN!

Materials

A bottle of lemonade (ideally cold, just like when you drink it)

4 or 5 Mentos (or as many as your dinner lady will give you)

Method

The thing about this experiment is that the moment the reaction starts you need to stand well back, unless you want to get soaking wet like me and Jake did. So a good way to drop all the Mentos in the bottle as quickly and smoothly as possible is to roll up a piece of paper into a tube, stick it down the mouth of the bottle and drop

---

* Not the one that's in your body. That's a thin tube about 10 cm long in the bottom-right corner of your abdomen and is part of your digestive system. This is just a section at the end of a book.

the Mentos in all at once. When you've done this, stand well back . . . maybe with an umbrella!

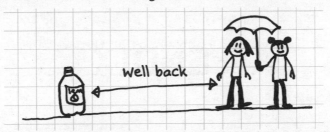

well back

And don't blame me if you get drenched in lemonade! Always do this outside with permission from whoever is in charge.

Results

Depending on the type of lemonade you use, you could end up with a lemonade fountain thats a couple of metres high. But beware, some brands will only get you 50 cm . . . Look on the bright side, at least you won't need that umbrella! Good luck!

Conclusion

Lemonade is really fizzy because it's a carbonated drink which means it has carbon dioxide dissolved in it. When you put in the Mentos the carbon dioxide (or CO_2 as I like to call it) gets released.

Because it's in a bottle it's held under pressure (much like I felt about the whole Brainbusters experience) and that's why it shoots out of the bottle foaming and bubbling, as all the pressure gets released (much like when we finally won Brainbusters!)

Because Mentos have a rough surface, unlike the smooth lemonade bottle, bubbles find it much easier to form so LOADS of them are made really quickly, just like a mini bubble factory!

There are SO MANY bubbles and they have nowhere else to go, so they just shoot right out

the bottle like molten lava in a volcanic eruption (only it's lemonade foam in a lemonade bottle eruption!).

Crazy, huh?!

HOW TO MAKE YOUR OWN SOLAR SYSTEM!

Materials

10 balls or spheres to represent your planets and the sun. (I used fruit and a sponge ball, but you can use anything that fits the bill. Polystyrene or modelling clay balls are probably the best as, unlike fruit, they don't rot, which I should probably have thought about before making my project! Your balls should be of differing sizes to best represent the relative size order of the planets and the sun — this is why I ended up using balls from as small as a peppercorn to as big as my yellow sponge ball.)

Glue (multipurpose glue is the best because it's pretty strong stuff)

Paint/varnish (or whatever you want to use to decorate your balls to make them more planet-like)

Large piece of black cardboard (this will be space . . . whoa!)

Gold or yellow cardboard (for cutting out your star shapes)

Scissors (also for cutting out your star shapes!)

Marker pen (for labelling your planets and writing any solar system or planet facts on your star shapes)

Sugar (to make your asteroid belt)

Glitter (for extra starry decoration)

Glue-stick (for sticking glitter and sugar, as multipurpose glue would be way too mucky for that)

Drawing pin and string (this will make a compass to draw perfectly circular orbits . . . clever, huh?)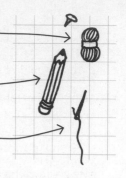

A pencil

Needle and thread (optional — for if you want to fix a sponge ball in the centre as your sun, like I did)

Method

The first thing you'll need to do is paint and varnish your planets if you're not happy with the way they already look. You'll need to leave these to dry overnight. That way you can sleep instead of being bored by literally watching paint dry!

Using the string, drawing pin and pencil, draw circular orbits for all your planets on the black cardboard, making sure you leave enough space within Mercury's orbit to stick the sun (every solar system needs a sun! We'd be lost without it!).

This can be done by pinning one end of the string with the drawing pin to the centre of your black cardboard and tying the pencil to the other end of the string so that the length of string is the radius of your first orbit (Mercury). By rotating the pencil around the drawing pin and holding the string taut, you will be able to draw orbit number one pretty easily.

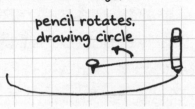

If you do it right you should have a perfect circle. Genius.

Increasing the length of the string each time by a small amount and repeating the process, you can draw orbits for all eight planets. You will need to make sure that your cardboard is big enough to fit all of these on before you start, otherwise you'll end up drawing on the table and being grounded. You might wind up on the green seats if you do it at school, so be careful!

Now you have your orbits, stick on your planets one by one, making sure you use the right size of ball for each planet. Multipurpose glue is best for this because it's multipurpose so it can be used for multiple purposes, including sticking planets onto card.

Now stick your sun in the centre of your solar system. If you are using a sponge ball, like I did, it doesn't stick very well with glue so maybe try sewing it on. You may need a friendly grown-up to help you with this.

If you want to add an asteroid belt, it goes in between Mars and Jupiter. Apply glue-stick between those two orbits and sprinkle on sugar. Sweet! You can sprinkle on glitter too for a bit of extra sparkle!

MARS

JUPITER

Not that kind of belt!

. . . the type with asteroids in!

If you want to add 'star facts', cut out some star shapes from your yellow or gold cardboard and write on facts about the solar system. You can find loads on the internet. My favourite fact was that Uranus has a battered moon called Miranda. I wonder who named it? Was their name Miranda? I hope they discover a moon and name it Cookie!

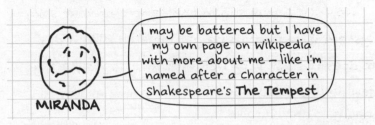

MIRANDA

I may be battered but I have my own page on Wikipedia with more about me – like I'm named after a character in Shakespeare's **The Tempest**

Label the planets with your marker pen and just in case you can't remember which is which . . . My Very Easy Method Just Speeds Up Naming Planets. Ha ha!

Results

You've now got your very own solar system! I bet it's not as good as mine. (It's probably better!!)

Conclusion

Your home-made solar system will help you remember the order of the planets. Cool, eh?

HOW TO MAKE A POTATO CLOCK
(Cookie-Style!)
Materials

Two potatoes (my favourite potatoes are Maris Pipers, but that's for making roast potatoes, not a potato clock)

Two short pieces of heavy copper wire (you can probably get this in a hardware store or maybe your parents have some knocking about in their toolkit)

Two nails (must be galvanised – this means coated in zinc and therefore able to act as a negative electrode – that's just like the minus side of a battery)

Three alligator clip leads (they are called this cos they have teeth just like alligators)

Small portable clock that uses only one AA battery

A marker pen

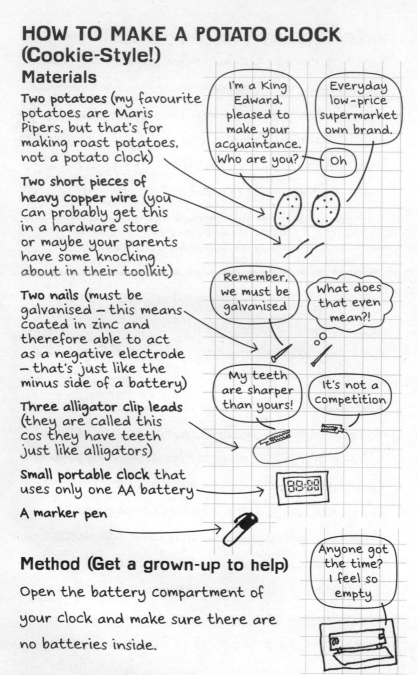

I'm a King Edward, pleased to make your acquaintance. Who are you?

Everyday low-price supermarket own brand.

Oh

Remember, we must be galvanised

What does that even mean?!

My teeth are sharper than yours!

It's not a competition

Anyone got the time? I feel so empty

Method (Get a grown-up to help)

Open the battery compartment of your clock and make sure there are no batteries inside.

238

Check that you know which are the positive and negative ends of the battery compartment. Just in case you have the same IQ as Suzie Ashby, the positive end is shown by the plus (+) sign and the negative end is shown by the minus (-) sign.

Draw a different face on each of your potatoes – one could be sad (your negative potato) and one could be smiley (your positive potato). Put a nail in each potato (now they're both sad! Joke! Potatoes don't have feelings!). Then put a copper wire into each potato as far away from the nails as possible.

Take one of the alligator leads and connect the copper wire in your happy potato to the positive (+) end of your clock's battery compartment. Then take another alligator lead and connect the nail in the sad potato to the negative (-) end of your battery compartment. Make sure that the alligator clip doesn't touch anything else metal apart from the positive (+) or negative (-) end of the battery compartment it's supposed to be connected to. Bit complicated, huh? But then again, we are creating an electrical circuit.

So far, we've only used two of our three alligator leads. Take the final alligator lead and clip one end to the nail in the happy potato and the other end to the copper wire in the sad potato.

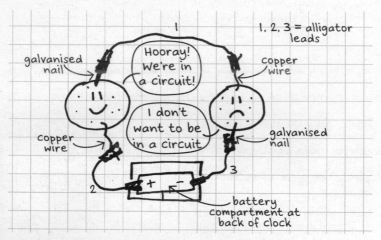

Results

This clock will tell the time as long as all the wires are connected properly. Hope you have a good time — ha ha ha!

Conclusion

The copper wire, the nails and the potatoes create an electric circuit that currents can run through, powering the clock. Isn't science awesome?

HOW TO MAKE A KALEIDOSCOPE!
(Cookie-Style!)

This is an alternative (and in my opinion, much cooler) version to the one Leo Mason made with a Pringles tube.

Materials

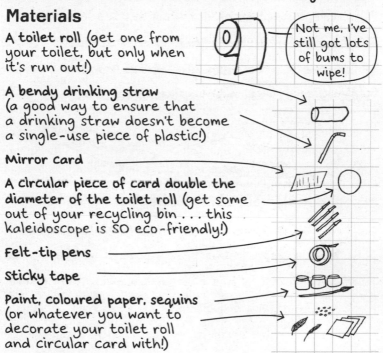

A toilet roll (get one from your toilet, but only when it's run out!)

Not me, I've still got lots of bums to wipe!

A bendy drinking straw (a good way to ensure that a drinking straw doesn't become a single-use piece of plastic!)

Mirror card

A circular piece of card double the diameter of the toilet roll (get some out of your recycling bin . . . this kaleidoscope is SO eco-friendly!)

Felt-tip pens

Sticky tape

Paint, coloured paper, sequins (or whatever you want to decorate your toilet roll and circular card with!)

Method

First, decorate the outside of your toilet roll. You can decorate your circular piece of card too. The more colourful, the better! The less colourful, the more boring!

BORING

WAY MORE FUN

Get your mirror card and fold it into a prism the same length as your toilet roll, making sure

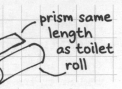

prism same length as toilet roll

the mirror side of the cardboard faces inwards.

Your prism should be the same shape as a Toblerone . . . the packaging not the actual chocolate, as that has indentations in it.

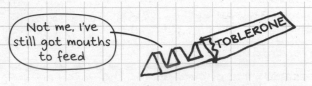

Not me, I've still got mouths to feed

TOBLERONE

Now insert your prism inside your toilet roll.

Next, take your bendy drinking straw and cut the long section so the bendy part is in the middle and both sections are the same length either side.

Use the sticky tape to stick the straw to your toilet roll so the bend is on the end of the roll.

Make a hole in the centre of your circle of cardboard and thread it onto the drinking straw so that the bendy section holds the circle of cardboard in place. In other words, your straw should be bent into an L-shape.

Same length (cut drinking straw)

drinking straw

loo roll

Straw threads on hole in circular card

Results

When you rotate your circle of cardboard (using the straw) and look through the end of your toilet roll it will make pretty, moving patterns. Yay!

Conclusion

When you look through the prism you'll only see a triangular section of your circular cardboard. However, the reflection on the three sides of mirror card will mean this view repeats so you have a symmetrical, ever-changing pattern as you rotate the cardboard circle with your hand. Pretty neat, right?

HOW TO MAKE PANCAKES!
(I learnt this in food technology!)

Materials

One mug (at home I have my own mug and I'm the only one allowed to use it. It says 'I love Cookies' on the side because it came in a gift pack with a tin of cookies. Sometimes I wish I could scrub out the 's'.)

One egg (did you know eggs can come in different colours depending on the hen that has laid them? You can even get green, blue and red eggs. Who knew?! Me! I knew! I wish that had come up on Brainbusters instead of blood plasma, which is definitely yellow!)

One greased frying pan (obviously greased with cooking oil as opposed to petroleum jelly or any other inedible grease!)

A fork (pretty self-explanatory)

A pinch of salt (also pretty self-explanatory)

A knob of melted butter (once again, pretty self-explanatory)

Milk (or you can use soya milk or almond milk)

Flour (you can use most types of flours but not Daisy Flowers because she's a floor assistant, not a cooking ingredient! For the best results, stick to plain flour.)

Spatula (this is one of my favourite words)

Wire cooling rack (optional)

Method

Pour the flour into the mug until it
is one-third full. You'd better not
be using my Cookie mug! Only I'm
allowed to use that – I don't want

your germs! Add milk till the mug is two-thirds
full. Then add the egg, the salt and the knob of
melted butter. Mix these in the mug with a fork.
There you go – that's your pancake mixture ready.
How easy was that?

You know how to do the rest – it's not rocket
science! Slowly pour some of the pancake mixture
into the greased frying pan and put it on a low
heat. Don't do this without a grown-up. Make a
nice batter circle. Once the first
side is cooked and bubbles have
started to form, you can
flip the pancake over with
a spatula and cook the

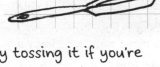

other side. You can also try tossing it if you're
confident it won't stick to the ceiling!

Use the spatula to lift your pancake out of
the pan and leave it to cool down on a wire grill.
Then repeat!

Results

Yummy!

Conclusion

Best served with

whipped cream,

strawberries, bananas, blueberries, chocolate sauce, maple syrup or just plain butter. Whatever you fancy, really! I quite like my pancakes with lemon and sugar.

OUT IN AUGUST 2020

COOKIE!

in her next adventure!

Turn the page
for an exclusive peek
at my new story!

CHAPTER 1

Spanner in The Works

Ugh, typical! Something always has to go wrong, doesn't it? Everything had been going so well since the beginning of the school year and the whole Jake thing. I mean, not getting on with Jake just seems like a 'blip' now!

It's weird to think how much I hated Jake at the beginning of the school term. Crazy weird! It's like *that* Jake was a different person from *this*

Jake then . . .

Jake now . . .

Jake. It's so easy to judge a book by its cover . . .

Hmm . . . This book has a boring cover — bet not much happens in it!!

Now I've got to know him properly he's GREAT and nothing like I thought back in those early days.

HIS DEEDS	MY THOUGHTS	
	THEN	NOW
Giving me some of his Dairy Milk	Ugh! He's trying to show how generous and kind he is	He's generous and kind and shares his Dairy Milk
Bringing homework round when I'm ill off school	Ugh! He's sucking up to my parents to show how studious he is	He's worried I'll get behind at school
Teaching me long words like DEFENESTRATE (to throw out of the window)	He's trying to outsmart me by saying long, cool words	He's helping me expand my vocabulary by saying long, cool words

Me, Jake and Keziah are like a little gang now. Hard to believe, because I've never been in a gang before and also cos I never thought anyone could come between me and Keziah. We've practically been joined at the hip for the last two years.

3

Before Keziah, I'd always been a bit of a loner.
Mum says that even when I was little, at playgroup,
all the other kids loved taking part in group
activities – singing nursery rhymes, doing all the
actions and joining in with story time – whereas I'd
always be doing my own thing at the back of the
class.

That's harder to do these days at school
considering I sit right near the front.

Actually, school is quite good at the moment.

Our head teacher, Mrs De Souza, is into science in a big way, so she's got us all interested in climate change and saving the planet, which personally I am all for because it's where I live.

I watched this documentary the other day and it showed how harmful plastics can be. Get this – every day approximately eight million pieces of plastic pollution find their way into the sea. Eight million!! That's more plastic in the sea than there are people

MEANWHILE IN THE BAHAMAS . . .

When the brochure said 'sea view' I didn't know it meant overlooking a rubbish tip

living in the whole of Scotland! Unbelievable!!!

So since then I've been making the whole family ditch single-use plastic, start recycling and generally be more environmentally friendly.

Dad, walk to the newsagent, don't drive

Mum . . . not using clingfilm again, are you?

Don't put that drinking straw in the bin!

Green box is for cardboard, blue is for bottles!

Keziah and Jake are both down with the whole eco-friendly thing too. Can you believe that a one-and-a-half degree rise in average temperature will have an irreversible effect on our planet?! Loads of different species would be wiped out!!

And it would be no good for us humans either. The sea levels would rise, land would be lost and millions of people would be made homeless. ALL because of one and a half degrees. How crazy! It sounds like nothing!

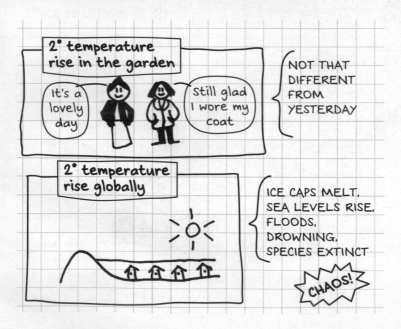

Let's make daisy chains

Hmm . . . I'm not sure where I stand on this environmentally. Daisies have feelings too . . . I think . . .

We try to be eco-friendly in everything we do now.

Keziah even cycled to mine today. Since she got her new bike,

her dads let her cycle over on her own at weekends, which is SO good – it's like being an independent grown-

Hooray, it's the weekend!

Yay! But it would be better if I could bend over . . .

up! We can practically spend all of Saturday and Sunday together. Bliss!

Thank goodness bikes don't have carbon emissions like cars do.

Hi!

Help! . . . I can't breathe!

Roubi (my middle sister) has a friend whose dad owns an electric car, which is *also* really good as it doesn't use any petrol and just runs on electricity instead. You plug it in to charge it as though it's a mobile phone or a tablet. How funny is that?!

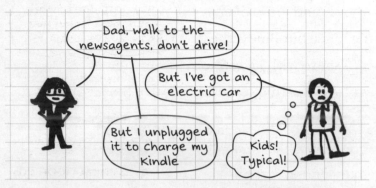

Roubi says it glides along without making any noise and often people don't hear it coming! In the future, all cars will be electric. They'll have to start making a special noise or there'll be a lot of squashed cats on the road!

Anyhow, me and Keziah are sitting in the garden discussing what I should do for my upcoming birthday, when who should jump over the fence but Bluey, the cat I share with Jake. She's

Lucky that lawnmower's so noisy . . . not like those electric cars — you just don't hear them, next thing you know, you've lost a life

probably getting out of the way of the lawnmower.

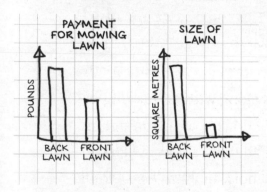

PAYMENT FOR MOWING LAWN

POUNDS

BACK LAWN FRONT LAWN

SIZE OF LAWN

SQUARE METRES

BACK LAWN FRONT LAWN

We can hear Jake cutting the grass next door. His parents pay him to do it, and at quite a good rate too. He gets ten pounds for the back lawn and five pounds for the front, which is WAY smaller. If you were going on price per area

he gets a much better deal on the front lawn as it's probably a tenth of the size of the back!

Mum, can I mow the front lawn now?

But you already did it five times this week — how about the back?

Err . . . actually it's OK

My parents
don't pay me to do
anything. I'm just
expected to do it all
for free! Slave labour,
if you ask me!

After Jake is finished, we all end up sitting in his
back garden making friendship chains with the
freshly-cut buttercups and daisies.

'Did you know daisies and buttercups are
actually weeds?' Keziah pipes up.

'My gran reckons a weed is just a plant in the
wrong place,' says Jake. 'It's only a weed if you don't
want it where it is.'

I've never thought of it like that but I guess that
if a rare orchid grew in the middle of a football
pitch then in a way it would be a weed because
you'd pull it out. You wouldn't want it there
disrupting the game!

'My gran says you can tell if people like butter by holding a buttercup under their chin and seeing if it shines yellow,' adds Keziah.

She tries it out on all of us, confirming we all like butter. I can't really add anything to the 'what our grannies say about buttercups and weeds' conversation as my Nani lives in Bangladesh and buttercups and daisies don't even grow there. Plus, she doesn't speak any English or even have Skype!

My mum gets long letters from her every now and then but I have no idea of her views on daisies and buttercups or what is and isn't a weed for that matter. But I could always add my own views to this conversation . . .

'The buttercup test is rubbish,' I declare. They stare at me so I have to back it up.

'It makes it seem like *everyone* likes butter, but surely not everyone in the whole world can!' I continue. 'What about people with a dairy intolerance?'

I did actually once google why buttercups are so shiny. I pretty much google everything these days, a habit I've got from Roubi, who often says 'Man's best friend is Google!'

'Buttercups are so shiny because they're trying to attract insects from a huge distance to pollinate them,' I explain to Jake and Keziah.

After I say it, I instantly realise how square I sound – it's like I just swallowed a textbook!

Luckily it seems to impress Keziah and even Jake, who remarks, 'With knowledge like that you should go on popular TV quiz show *Brainbusters!*' We all laugh.

It's starting to get dark outside and Keziah suggests we go in. Keziah has been scared of the dark ever since I can remember. She still sleeps with a night light on, whereas I need pitch-black darkness to sleep. The first time I stayed over at Keziah's, I couldn't sleep all night because of her annoying night light.

I can remember watching her Winnie the Pooh alarm clock and counting down the hours till morning. I've got used to sleeping at hers since then.

'Nah, let's stay out longer,' says Jake. 'You've got to conquer your fears face-on.'

'Bet you wouldn't think that if *you* were scared of something,' I say.

'Nothing scares me,' he replies defiantly.

'Everyone's scared of something,' says Keziah. '*Please* can we go in now?'

After some protesting by Jake that his room is too messy for visitors and that the beautiful outdoors should be appreciated at night, he finally relents and we go inside. We sneak past his mum, who is watching a crime drama, and head up to his bedroom. Jake's mum can talk for England and because she's never met Keziah before, if we had bumped into her it would have been a good two hours before we got away.

And your great, great, great grandparents — what did they do for a living?

?

As we head to Jake's room, I notice a load of half-packed suitcases in his parents' bedroom.

Keziah asks him if they are going away and Jake tells us that his dad is taking his little brother on a trip to Disneyland as a treat for his birthday. Jake's family are SO cool. We NEVER do stuff like that in our family. I can't imagine getting a trip to Disneyland as a birthday present. That would be off the scale!

'Yay, tickets to Disneyland!'

'Oh . . . it's just a colouring book . . . BAH'

Jake's bedroom is really fun to hang out in. It's kind of cosy with dark walls plastered with posters over every square centimetre, and a thickly carpeted floor. There are loads of gadgets and

gizmos too. Jake is currently into Aliana Tiny – he has *all* her music and can do *all* the dance moves from *all* her videos.

Jake is a really good dancer. Me and Keziah are both rubbish. Unlike most kids our age, we're not really into Aliana Tiny. She's playing Wembley Stadium soon and all the tickets sold out in the FIRST HOUR! They're pretty much like gold dust.

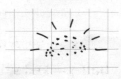

Knowing Jake's parents, they've probably already got him a pair as a surprise.

Front lawn's great, darling. Do the back and we'll get you a private box at Aliana . . .

We plonk ourselves down on Jake's bed. Jake has a DOUBLE bed, which is pure luxury. He reckons it's because he has to give up his room if relatives come to stay but that's probably only once a year, if that, so he really *is* getting a good deal. No one else in our class has their OWN double bed. Not even Suzie Ashby. A double bed wouldn't even *fit* in my room!

Maybe it'll fit if I get rid of my desk and wardrobe?

Double bed sticking out my bedroom door

Keziah looks around. 'Wow! You have so much stuff,' she says. 'All this plastic can't be good for the environment!'

Stuff like us Lego bricks are used lots so we're OK! It's these pesky single-use things like sweet wrappers you gotta look out for!

At least we're not annoying to step on in bare feet!

'But it's not single-use, like a carrier bag or drinking straw,' Jake protests. 'None of this is going in the bin any time soon.'

'True.' Keziah smiles. 'I've never seen so much stuff though. Your room is like Aladdin's cave!'

'Just birthday presents and bits and pieces that have built up over the years,' he replies.

That reminds me I have to decide what I'm doing for my birthday, which is coming up soon. I never usually do anything for it but this one's the big 1-0. I'll be an entire *decade* old! One tenth of a century! Double figures! We all decide that we'll get thinking of a good way to celebrate.

'OMG! Am I taking my whole class to Disneyland?'

'No, Roubi and Nahid didn't want their colouring books!'

'When is it exactly?' Jake asks.

'Two Saturdays' time,' I reply.

'That's when Suzie Ashby's birthday party is,' says Jake. 'She's inviting everyone in the class, apparently. I heard her telling Alison Denbigh. She reckons she's even getting a party planner.'

Keziah bursts out laughing. 'What? That's a bit grand, isn't it!? Where's she holding it? The Ritz?!'

Great. Suzie Ashby is having a party with the whole class at the Ritz – on MY birthday. How can I compete with that? I'll have to think of something, and fast . . .